CARAVAN

CARAVAN

MARTIN KEAVENEY

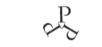

PENNILESS PRESS PUBLICATIONS
www.pennilesspress.co.uk/books

Published by
Penniless Press Publications 2022

ISBN 978-1-913144-39-5

Cover Image: Paul Butler

For Mam

1

In the darkest corner of the caravan Gus sits when he hears the vehicle in the distance. He takes one last look around and leaves the peculiar small world it offers and steps out into the sunlight and the leafy wood.

He can recognise the unusual driving – the stopping, the starting, the pulling in, the pulling out. The residents of the area plodded along at thirty miles an hour. Never too fast that they wouldn't be able to scan neighbours' fields, never too slow that they would be beeped at from behind. He sits outside the caravan on a battered beer crate, in front of a small fire of kindling, preparing a suitably morose expression.

Early in the morning he had put the final touches to the set-up: a jar of old coffee he had been preserving from the bin specially, some stale bread, a pile of conkers awaiting shelling on the draining board, a home-made fishing rod. The bed covered in a torn and stained duvet. Toilet arrangements he decided not to leave evidence of, fully prepared to explain his moveable latrine technique, if it was called upon. A chair with a hole in the seat was ready in this event behind the caravan.

The new car came into view. A shiny blue model finding its way now, crunching the gravel beneath. Gus' eyes open as the warmth develops in the pit of his stomach like simmering honey. The sweet nectar of pounds, pennies and pence. Or whatever name the beurocrats gave it nowadays.

She parks in front of the caravan. His imported Mitsubishi Lancer is safely tucked a mile away behind his parent's stone cottage at the edge of the forest. All that is visible as a mode of transport are his hiking boots, ripped, one side leaking, a piece of baling twine substituting as a lacer. There is also a High Nelly bicycle – the old black 'man's bike', with back wheel suitably flat and frame generally rusted and somewhat rickety. She waves a restrained salute as she arrives. His face broadens, it is like his whole body widens out, like an accordion, in a welcoming gesture. As though pleased to see anyone in this wilderness.

Gus gets up from the stool, walking over to meet the official. She looks at him through the window, smiling, as she takes up her case. Some files slide out and she delays opening the car door to put them back in. You can leave them, he thinks.

'Mr. Watt, I take it,' she says as she emerges, outstretching a nail-painted hand.

'Howya,' Gus replies, shaking the hand.

'It's a pleasure,' she says.

'Come,' he turns to the caravan.

She speaks with an educated accent he dislikes almost at once. He leads her to the door of the caravan.

'So this is your hideaway,' she says casually.

'Oh, it's no hideaway,' Gus says, matter-of-factly. He enters the caravan and his boots make sticking noises on the lino. He turns sadly. 'This is home,' he declares, perhaps too dramatically.

She enters, lowering her head, as though there might not be enough head space.

'Please, sit,' he points to a three-legged chair, which has a piece of garden post replacing the fourth leg. He stands awkwardly near the door, blocking a large proportion of light.

'Thank you. Well, Mr.Watt, I'm Mary Kilroy from Support Services–'

'Gus, you can call me. Cup of tea?'

'Eh, I don't mind.'

'Actually, I don't have any tea. Coffee?'

'That will be fine, yes.'

'Okay, hold on and we'll see what we can do.'

'So, I was saying, we received your application and as you know–'

'I just have to go down to the well.' Gus is looking vaguely out the door through the dense trees beyond.

'Sorry?'

'Just to get some water, I'm an awful man, should have prepared better, feck it.'

'Really, Mr.Watt, it's fine.'

He looks suddenly at the kitchenette area. 'Oh. I have a bottle here. There's a bit of luck. Hold on now the fire is coming along nicely.'

He plucks a blackened pot from the tiny sink and slowly fills it with a coke bottle of water. He brings it outside to the smouldering pile of sticks. He places the pot gently on top, stoking until a small flame flickers.

'Won't be long' he says, coming back into the caravan, sitting on the narrow sofa bed.

'It's quite alright, Mr.Watt. Now...'

He hears no more. He is looking at her eyes as they read the words from the page in front of her. Eyes with large pupils like round bales. Perfectly circular. They would roll him into a frenzy. He fights a sudden image of the woman in lingerie. Miss– Miss Kilroy, yes.

This was unexpected.

Her inky black hair is tied back. He wonders what it would be like to unfurl it.

'...entitlements and other essentials–' Miss Kilroy is saying.

'Did you say your name was Mary?' Gus asks suddenly, when Miss Kilroy is in mid-sentence saying the word 'disadvantaged.'

'Eh, yes. Why?'

She looks at him directly as though there is obviously some practical reason for this interruption such as: his cousin is called Mary; he watched a programme on his non-existent television about someone called Mary; his great Uncle was mistaken for a woman and called Mary. Any of the above.

'The pot is boiled,' Gus says.

He brings it in and fills two fishermen's enamel mugs he takes from a press with a squeaking door. He drops in two spoons of coffee.

'I'm afraid I've no milk. Do you take sugar?'

'No thanks, that will be fine.'

'I don't have any, anyways.'

He hands her the barely mixed liquid. Granules float around in the mug. 'Thank you.'

'Sandwich?'

'No, thank you.'   Just as well. The rim of the mug scorches Miss Kilroy's tongue and she turns red. 'Oh!'

'Too hot, sorry. Them cups aren't the best. Fishermen's you see. For worms really.' The drop she had in her mouth jets out.

'I'm so sorry, Mr. Watt, it's quite hot.'

'I'm sorry, I'm sorry, too. I'll mop that up.'

He gets a filthy rag he uses for cleaning burnt oil off the tractor and is playing the part of dish dryer in this scene. Gus notices Miss Kilroy's shoulders have drooped slightly. He senses some of the official haughtiness has been abandoned through the mug episode. He hadn't expected her posterior to be quite such a palatable shape. He would have preferred now to have brought one of the armchairs from the cottage. However, comfort had not been the image he wanted to present.

'So Mr. Watt, you are living here how long?'

'Ten years.'

'I see. And where were you before that?'

'That would all be on the system.'

Stunning looking bundle of flesh or not, she was still a civil servant and had to be handled with care. No need to make it too easy for them.

'Yes, I know Mr.Watt, but for our department records you see.'

Her voice has a balanced official air to it as she rhymes off the interrogation the state pays her to do, her hair, somewhat trapped amongst the loose pony–tail, bounces around her shoulders. Gus wants to hear her speak in a different tone – in that lilting touch of northern airs he can hear hidden beneath the corporate mask, making warm cooing noises as he rolls an ice cube around her chest.

'And why did you leave the cottage your parents live in?'

'Arragh,' Gus says, dismissively. 'You couldn't live there. They told me I had to leave.' Her delicate eyebrows climb up her forehead slightly. 'Go down and ask them,' he adds.

'That won't be necessary.'

'It was too small. And then there was the bad blood.'

'Sorry?'

'Bad blood.' Gus sips from the liquid. A coffee granule sticks to his upper lip. He quickly licks it off with his tongue. 'They gave the farm to my brother.'

Miss Kilroy crunches her nose. 'Oh. I see. That's fine, Mr.Watt. Now, how have you been supporting yourself?'

'Well, the state payment. Good to have it, I know. But it's a small amount here in the winter when you have nawthin''. He emphasises the word 'nawthin'' as though he is tearing a piece of iron with his teeth.

'Quite.'

'Are you a local girl yourself?' Gus asks.

'Not originally. I'm from a small island up north…'

'Oh yeah…fairly wild up there.'

11

'Hmmm. Now, it appears this wood is owned by the state. So you would in effect be squatting, is that correct?'

The interview went on for ninety minutes. Every question he could think of she asked and many more. Where did he get his water? Where did he get his fuel? How did he deal with sewage? How did he deal with rubbish? Did he intend the caravan to be a permanent abode in the future? State regulations, she explained, turning a page efficiently. He notes her fingernails are unpainted, sharp, tasty. They would dig deep into the back of a man at certain moments. He walks her out to the car.

 'So you live local, then?' he says bluntly. This was as obvious as he could get away with. The county town is the response.

 'Mmm. Where do you go for a drink then?'
 'Oh, it depends. Nice to meet you, Mr.Watt.'
 'Bojo's is the main spot there now I think.'
 'I suppose it is.'
 'Saturday night is the big night there.'
 'Good bye, Mr.Watt.'
 'See you.'

Back at the cottage, Gus is distracted. His mind is full of the rugged island up north, strict but alluring dark-haired women, ice cubes. His reality is deaf parents, a radio show at maximum volume, a rotting turf shed roof. Drops of stale rain roll down the back of his neck as he fills a former fertiliser bag with awkwardly shaped sods. In his small bedroom, after a plate of bacon and cabbage, he tries to put things into words. He sits on his bed with a pen and his notebook. Sometimes a poem will provide a relief from the insatiable…

 He muses while looking out his window at the box hedge he was supposed to cut weeks ago. Officials, officials. Guards, teachers, traffic wardens. Yes, they seem to make him feel agitated. What is it, he wonders? He writes 'The Official'. Nothing arrives to follow. He muses for a few moments. At the bedroom door, his mother reminds him of her afternoon appointment at the Doctor.

Dr. White's clinic is an old building he was brought to as a child. The secretary is a woman of few words and a steel personality. The room is cold. His mother leafs through a magazine on the table screaming with remarkable family scenarios and bizarre medical occurrences. Mrs. Hook arrives, a pinched woman of seventy.

'Hello Mrs. Watt, how are you?'

'Well, I'm not too bad, it's my foot giving me trouble again.'

'Arragh, sure these doctors, do they know what they're doing at all, at all?'

'Well, I don't know…'

The secretary leans over the counter. 'Mrs. Watt, you can see the nurse first.'

The door is opened and Gus' mouth is open for some seconds before he realises. It is like St. Peter's gate except a female angel is there instead of the bearded saint. Her blonde hair tied back and her blue eyes dazzling in a white uniform make Gus feel a strange, pleasant pain. He cannot help but run his eyes up and down her body with perfect curves and honey-shaped hips: if honey had a shape, it would be the shape of this nurse's hips. He remembers hearing her scowling, bucket-jawed predecessor had retired, and a replacement was rumoured to have arrived from the east. The big white door is shut and the vision is gone. Gus feels a need to breathe deeply.

There you go. You work away for years on mad women on the wrong side of the biological clock frantically looking to reproduce, fed-up housewives looking for a bit of excitement, just legal freshers who didn't even know the mechanics of a buckle belt. And then along comes two in a week. In a day. These two could be mad too, but…no. They worked in state jobs. They were conformists. And they could conform to him, too.

He has photographically memorised the nurse's right ring finger, bare as the day it was born. Gus takes one of the woman's magazines and tries to take his mind off the new nurse. Every page she is there, in every feature, her lovely face, her big blue eyes. Not nicer than Miss Kilroy's, but different, a special sea blue deepness in them, he wants to get into the water of them and swim. He knows he will have to ask the nurse about his mother, something about her, anything. How to tune the hearing aid maybe, how to adjust the length of her aluminium walking stick to address a sudden increase in the stoop trajectory. What is it this week – ah yes, the bunion. How exactly should Mrs. Watt apply the cream? She may not have understood your instructions. Anything which would ease his voice and face into her consciousness, anything to show her he was here and he was interested. Then he would know by her body language whether there was a chance, a possibility.

Maybe the feeling will go off him, he might have imagined her loveliness, she may not be that beautiful at all. He hears the white door opening and can already hear her sweet tone of voice. Mrs. Hook is in the door before he can make any comment on the session, but the flash of the nurse's features is enough to confirm his first impression.

He thinks about the nurse on the way home. Her name is Needham. She is from the city, his mother confirms. Newly arrived in the town. A lovely girl. Very polite. Didn't even need the doctor. Gave a good cream for the bunion.

In the afternoon, Gus cruises around the town, paying particular attention to the clinic. At four o'clock the door closes. He parks across and sits there, daydreaming.

After an hour he goes into The Red Oak, from where he can see the entrance to the clinic. A slumped figure, Reilly, snores at the corner of the bar.

'How are you, Gus?' Liam says, arriving from the cellar room. Gus orders a pint of beer. Miss Needham emerges and sits into a sleek two-door hatchback.

'Leave, that Liaming, will ya…'

'Hah?' The middle-aged proprietor says shakily in mid pull, the ease of his existence somehow shook.

Gus' eyes follow the hatchback as he gets to his car. Miss Needham drives up the street and stops outside the supermarket. Gus drives up in front of her car. No escape, he thinks. In the street, the old couple who sit in their car all day observing the comings and goings of the locals watch him closely. He wanders casually into the supermarket. Grannies buying midweek shopping. A drunken man toys with himself in the drinks' aisle. Three youths wander around, one wearing a man's fishing cap, speaking loudly and distracting the cashiers so they can pick up bits and pieces and toss them into their boxers. No one checks the boxers.

He spots her at the freezer, taking up a small tub of dairy ice cream. He looks at the trolley, a small carry basket. Within are a single person's purchases: a small tub of pâté, some lettuce, a cleaning agent. A few things. Living on her own. He rubs his hands. He takes up a loaf to be on a pretext, in the event of her looking up and adopts a suitably casual air. Now the difficult part. The intentional 'unintentional' interception. He is about to walk toward her when a giant shadow arrives and his vision is completely obscured.

'Augey, how are things!' Franny Morrin offers a large hand.

'Hello, Fran...' Gus' tone is marginally homicidal. But Franny is totally oblivious and motors straight into a detailed description of his search all over town for a good weedkiller. 'I think they are diluting them, Augey!'

Franny is in a select group that salute him as 'Augey,' which also includes his brother Stephen, and his manically depressed aunt in north London.

'You know I sprayed the road in March and here I am in August pulling up new weeds! And it's supposed to work for eighteen months, hah?'

'Really?'

An engine starts on the street. Gus looks around sharply and sees Miss Needham drive off into the rainy sunset. Franny is muttering something about football as Gus leaves the shop.

It is early next morning when he wakes. The bog is quiet: the local effort at the dawn chorus is somewhat haphazard. McCluskey arrives at seven, a tingling noise coming from his exhaust for some miles back. The morning news blares though the half-open driver's window. Gus quickly butters two cuts of bread and laces them with ham. McCluskey will have a kettle. He grabs a few teabags.

The van is still cold. McCluskey slurps on a large mug of tea, its steam and his morning breath intermingling and surrounding his large head in a thick fog. Conversations are limited for the first half hour as they make their way through the winding road north. Eventually the questions begin. First, as always, innocent seeming:

'How did you get on yesterday?'

'Oh, good, good.'

A long pause. Then: 'Did you get your business done?'

'I did.'

Too late he realises business is a clue: business was not something he had made obvious before. Business could mean money or strokes, probably both. Even McCluskey could appreciate affairs of the loins were not termed as business.

'Did you buy?' McCluskey says eventually, unable to contain himself, as they reach the job, this week in a small village amongst the mountains.

'Buy what?'

'Whatever you were buying.'

'Who says I was buying anything?'

'Are you changing the car?'

'Do we need milk?' Gus says, making shapes to get out of the van as they approach a shop on the quiet village street.

The site is abandoned. The two carpenters, who were tacking drywall boards to ceilings before Gus took his mysterious day off, have not arrived yet. McCluskey's shakes his head in disgust. 'Imagine. Half eight and no sign. And us coming fifty miles. Them fellas are only down the road, hah?'

'They're right, what is the bleddy panic?' Gus says, which provokes a blasphemed facial response from his employer.

McCluskey whistles as he mixes a half bucket of bonding, ground up rock and chemicals with water. He snaps some aluminium bead and deftly sticks them around the window frame with the pink mix. They will be set within half an hour. Gus gets on with the mix, thirty to forty shovels of sand, a bag of cement, three caps of waterproofer. The mix needs to be pliable and sticky but not watery. While the mixer does its job, Gus goes into the house, and gets the board and stand ready. The board is a jagged piece of plywood, the stand is one of the few proper pieces of equipment McCluskey has, an actual mortar stand, although battered and caked with old concrete. 'Where are you starting?'

17

'In here,' McCluskey replies from the last bedroom at the end of the hall.

It is strange to think of a family eventually living in the houses they plaster, where now they plod around in heavy steel-toe boots and criticise other trades, Gus often thinks. He sets up the board.

'So what did you buy?' McCluskey says casually, as he marginally adjusts the angle bead with the window frame. He continues to eye the line, tapping the bead with his trowel, without looking at Gus, who tries to avoid lumps of concrete that the block layers failed to remove on the ground.

'Yeah,' he replies and walks off to the mixer.

'Don't be like that,' McCluskey shouts, grinning to himself, scraping a rogue piece of bonding off the windowsill.

'You're right there.'

The room is partially plastered by ten o'clock. McCluskey works the hawk and trowel with the ease of years' practice, a slick sweep of the trowel devours the defenceless blocks, covered forever more. At a certain stage he reaches for the long aluminium straight edge and flattens the covered wall, neatly scraping it down to a half-inch thickness. He then carefully fills the holes where the depth is too thin and slides the edge across again.

'There must be a woman involved,' McCluskey announces as Gus enters with his tenth barrow.

'What did you say?' Gus says, slanting his head toward the large round shape at the wall, shovel somewhat threateningly raised off the ground.

'Oh, nawthin', nawthin',' McCluskey replies, with glinting eyes shining, even in the dull light of the half-plastered room.

In the evening, Gus is tired. McCluskey cleans his tools under the running water of the temporary supply, a long piece of three-quarter inch pipe which must be kinked in the absence of a tap. 'You won't say, no?'

'It's going to rain tonight.' Gus tosses the wheelbarrow into the back of the van.

'Don't forget the drill tomorrow,' Gus says, as they reach the little cottage. Otherwise they will be using the old-fashioned and labour intensive plunger, a rough implement with a long handle which is used to mix the skimcoat plaster. McCluskey's drill is attached to a whisk which makes light work of this task.

'We'll need the generator then and I'll have to get petrol,' McCluskey replies, with the tone of a child who has just had a circus visit cancelled.

'Well, bring it then.'

'I don't know why you want that, sure I'll only need a few buckets,' McCluskey mutters, driving off before Gus could reply.

'Bring it,' Gus shouts, after the jangling van, 'the drill!'

2

In the morning, McCluskey arrives without the drill to the fury of his labourer. A motor is gone in it, he claims, his owl-like eyes opening wide as he says the word 'gone'. Gus heaves bags of skimcoat over to the old plastic bucket once used for tile grout. He carefully pours the ground-up rock and chemical mixture into the half bucket of water, slowly mixing it with a stick until the consistency is of curdled butter. He takes up the plunger and, sweating with exertion, runs it through the mix quickly, absorbing the lumps into the skim. He eases the smooth mixture onto the board set up in the middle of the floor.

'You see, you don't need the drill, you're a dab hand.'

'Jays, Pat did you ever think of going on the road?

'Whaddya mean?'

'With your stand-up routine?' Gus says, scraping the skim out.

McCluskey sweeps a hawkful away and proceeds to coat the fresh sand and cement walls he plastered the day before. As he coats, he whistles. 'So how is the caravan?'

'What are you saying?' Gus says as he leaves the room to mix another bucket.

When he returns, McCluskey continues. 'Are you moving into the wood?' A big guffaw.

Reilly was the culprit. McCluskey often dropped into the Red Oak for a pint on a Thursday evening. Reilly, in a rare moment of clarity, had seen Gus travelling through the village with the caravan from the midlands on Tuesday night, the whistling noise of a banjaxed rim drawing him into the sad world of reality. 'How come the wheel was flat?'

'Yer man left if flat.'

'And why didn't ya pump it?'

'Couldn't fit the valve, what's it to ya?'

'Aright, I'm only asking. Was there no adaptor?'

'He didn't give me the adaptor.'

'Oh. You must have done him so.'

'Is it teatime?

With a perceptiveness of years' practice, McCluskey had deduced correctly. Gus had stubbornly negotiated the price down and the seller was so infuriated he had taken the final offer without a word and driven off. It was sometime later Gus realised he had also kept the vital tyre adaptor. Gus had well-earned the two hundred euros he had knocked off the price in the sixty miles from the scrap yard, the rim screeching, leaving a chalk line clearly tracking his progress, all the way up through the main street of the town.

Later, McCluskey, with his trowel and a wet brush, flattens the hardwall and deftly skims with the trowel to achieve a glassy finish. Already dark blotches are appearing as the wall dries out.

'Are you going moving in to it?' he repeats his question with a small modification.

'I just wanted something in case.'

'In case of what?'

'Where do you want these planks?'

'Are you going on holidays with it?'

'Hah! No.'

'What do you want it for then?'

'I'll throw them outside, will I?'

'Do please. Well?'

Gus, having no energy for thinking of any lies, walks out of the room and cleans old hardwall off his jeans. Dangerous to let the Owl man know anything of his plans. Wouldn't agree with, with the principles of it. McCluskey is proud of his virginal status with the courts. 'Never been in one of them places,' he is fond of telling Gus during turbulent periods in his labourer's life.

It is half six when McCluskey pulls up at the end of Gus' road.

'Them flats in Killabilloo won't be ready for a week or two.'

'That place is an awful length away.'

'We'll have to wait in it.'

'I'm not staying in Killabilloo!'

Gus gets out of the van clutching the fifties McCluskey had handed him.

'We can stay in your caravan, sure you could go touring in that yoke,' McCluskey shouts out the window.

'Sunday night at the Gaiety for you Pat, definitely,' Gus says in a roar.

On Saturday morning Gus tidies up around the cottage. There are some weeds cracking through. He clears a blocked gulley. He brings in some turf from the shed. His father coughs and tells him that the sods are wet. 'That old roof is leaking.'

Gus examines it from the doorway. There is no excuse he can think of. 'I could change a few of the sheets, I suppose.'

'I didn't mean you to make a frog's umbrella of it. Get Twomey.'

'That fella'd rob ya.'

'What do you know about roofs?'

In the kitchen, Gus bangs the turfbox down. His father does not hear this. He fiddles with his hearing aid.

Gus drives into town at lunchtime and places a bet on a race at three thirty in Keane's Bookies. He waves at the couple sitting in the car. They look worried. He enters The Postman lounge and drinks a pint of beer. He buys a newspaper. He returns to Keane's. His horse finished eighth.

At five he returns and with a step ladder, climbs up onto the roof. His father appears at the door. 'Where are you going, did you call Twomey?'

'Will you go inside, will ya!'

'Quare time of the day to start work'.

'I'm just having a look.'

The small stepladder wobbles as Gus reaches the summit, looking beyond a wrinkled y-front. The roof is in urgent need of attention. The galvanize sheets have mostly rusted through. The circles around each washer have in places expanded as rust eats into the sheet. Beneath, most of the rafters look sound enough. He looks back across the sheets again. In other areas, the screws and washers have corroded together, seeming to melt into one tormentingly-difficult-to-remove headache. He frowns, his neck becomes itchy. No route out of this predicament arrives. But he could not have the wisecracking Twomey criticising the roof, the roof he clad fifteen years earlier as a token of penance after the debacle on the peninsula.

Bojo's is a large super pub in the main county town. Gus rarely comes here, a sprawling place on a Saturday night, miniskirts and open shirts, sweat and cigarette smoke, bad pints and arguments. He pushes through the heaving crowd, holding a small bottle of Budweiser. His Diesel shirt is soft on his skin; his sister, Theresa, brought it from England. A chain with a crucifix dangles from his neck. The pub is stone clad on the inside, creating an echoey atmosphere. The clink of glasses consistently battles with the music for supremacy. He wanders around for an hour; there is no sign of Miss Kilroy. He sits at the counter looking at the youths, all fifteen years younger than him. He then remembers the bar, and that he is in the lounge.

Through the glass door he sees her sitting with a less attractive friend at the counter. She is drinking tonic water. They are turned toward the bar. She wears a white dress. Her hair is tied back. He can see her shoulders, brown, nicely tanned. He looks in the mirror under the optics. Her bust is large and the top of her breasts are clearly visible. Gus begins to lose his breath. Out of the official armoury she is even more desirable. He goes down to the toilet, negotiating his way around two heated arguments and a man philosophizing with a cigarette machine. He tosses some water on his face and wipes it with toilet paper. He tries to tidy his balding head. He adopts a casual but strong expression. He straightens his suede jacket which makes no difference but he feels more comfortable. Now. Now he is ready.

The glass door squeaks as it opens, and Miss Kilroy and her less attractive friend look around. 'How are ye?' Gus says, smiling.

'Hello.'

'Hello, Mary.'

'Augustus, how are you? This is my friend, Tanya.'

'Hello. Can I get you a drink?'

They pause and eventually accept. He sips his bottle of beer. 'Busy crowd out there.'

'Yeah, we were taking refuge.' Her smile goes through him like some kind of relentless missile. He is floating up off the ground into the ceiling of the bar. The barman, who presents a soured-milk expression, considers him icily. There is a need for Gus to pull himself back into the moment.

'Are you a local woman?' he asks Tanya and then immediately regrets it. What is he asking about Tanya for; does he want to give the lovely Mary the wrong idea? Yet he cannot look at her directly, he is afraid her eyes will hold him there and he will be staring like a stunned sheep.

'I work with Mary,' Tanya is explaining. Gus is careful to maintain a present but non overtly influential presence in the flow of dialogue. He gently negotiates a quiet but effective and non-judgemental presence through subjects he knows nothing about such as the civil service, holidays in Majorca and sociological developments in the country, which is what the two women seem to have in common.

'Will you be around my village again?' Gus asks after a while.

'Tuesday as it happens,' she says, her eyes glinting in the yellow glow. 'I've a few meetings along the coast.'

'Do you fancy a bowl of soup in The Postman on your way home?' Gus says, with the tone of telling a joke. However, he makes himself hold her gaze this time, to confirm his genuineness.

The sun shines on Sunday. The village church is the modern design. It has a triangular footprint surrounded by well-manicured grounds. Floor to ceiling glass panels form part of the walls. Gus stands at the back. Along the low windowsill sit many of the town's bachelors: Twomey, O'Leary, even Reilly has managed to put in an appearance. Reilly's counterpart in The Postman, Dunleavy, is not present, his religious preference is unknown. The priest warns of complacence. Gus sees McCluskey in the distance. The plasterer sits with his wife and six daughters.

Gus' mother serves charred roast beef with lumpy potatoes. Gus spends the day reading the *Sunday World*. In the evening, he makes another attempt at his poem, 'The Official'. No words come. He goes to bed early.

Next morning, there is still no news from McCluskey, so he decides to tackle the shed after a boiled egg and jam buttered toast. Still the job does not really interest him. It is the start, he tells himself. Get stuck in. That was what they were told at football training many years ago. But he could never catch the other players to 'get stuck in'.

He searches his old tool box in vain for a suitable pinch bar. Eventually, armed with only the bent remains of a tractor stabilising lever, he reaches the roof. The nails are screwed in tightly. Ah yes, he had a good drill that time. Where had that gone? He smashes the heads with the bar. He tries to prise the first sheet up with a number of the screws still in place. This is not successful. He grunts

'You know fierce rain is promised?' his father says in a croak from the back door.

'Didn't hear about that.' Gus grunts as he wrestles with the sheet which eventually comes partly away, leaving a small triangle of galvanise still obstinately remaining. Only thirty nine more sheets to go.

At five o'clock Gus positions himself at the front window of The Red Oak. This time he gets to drink the first pint. The news announces further cutbacks.

'Bastards,' Liam says, turning the volume to mute as he wipes the inside of the counter. The nurse emerges from the side door of the clinic. Gus swallows the last drop of beer. Again, he drives up the street toward Joyce's minimarket. Today, there is no sign of Franny. There is no time to lose.

He finds Miss Needham selecting aubergines at the small vegetable section.

'You want to be careful with them,' Gus says, smiling.

'Why is that?' she asks.

'They spray them with bleddy chemicals. I'd wash them if I were you...'

'Really?' she answers, smiling he notes.

'You work in the clinic,' Gus declares.

'I do.'

'Yeah. My mother goes there. Watt.'

'Oh, yeah. Lovely woman.'

Really? Try being her son. 'Are you staying in the town?'

'Yeah, just out the road.'

'Oh. Well. See you again.'

'See you.'

That night he dreams of Miss Kilroy and Miss Needham somehow agreeing with their presence under his blankets. The fantasy is hampered somewhat by the booming soundtrack of *Bonanza* which his father decides to start watching at two o'clock in the morning.

After another more leisurely breakfast, he returns to the roof. Five sheets lie in unrecognizable form in the yard, the remaining still tightly clinging to the rafters.

'Why did you go at that this week, do you know there is thunder promised?' his father says in a growl from the kitchen door.

'What thunder? I didn't hear of any thunder. Anyways, it won't take long…'

'Twill the way you're goin' about it…'

His father sniffs, patting his behind as he turns back inside. After dinner Gus feels lethargic. Muttering something about nails, he drives into the town. The street is quiet at two on a Tuesday. He wanders around for an hour spending some time scanning *The Dealer* in Joyce's. While he is estimating how reliable the advertised mileage is in an '83 Escort, he glimpses Miss Needham passing along the street. Sauntering out for a half hour break between appointments, no doubt. Golden locks reflecting sunlight. He hurries out. She slows at the window of a dress shop. Casually he saunters up behind her.

'They're a bit pricey in there,' Gus says nodding at the dressed mannequins.

'An expert, are you?' she smiles. Ah yes, smiling again.

'Not really. So the old lady says.' She laughs. They always laugh at a reference to his mother. 'Where do you go for the lunch?'

Women of this class do not partake in one o'clock bacon and cabbage. They prefer Paninis, goat's cheese, crepes. Whatever that muppet running the Country Kitchen out of his uncle's farm can toss out.

'I just bring sandwiches, actually.' The city feel is found in the 'actually' phrase. Nice. Different.

'Well, they do a good sandwich in The Red Oak if you ever fancy one.'

'Well, I'll keep that in mind.'

She is gone. He feels sad.

They sit in the corner of The Postman. He looks at her clothes, a tight blue jeans and cool white blouse. She must have changed; this was not the work suit he had met her in. This was exciting. Miss Kilroy has a soft face, warm. She speaks in a less officious tone now. She asks him about himself, about the village, about life in general. It is so difficult to find words to use without wishing to impress. He avoids talking about cattle, sprayers, fishing licenses and their general avoidance.

'I like your outfit,' he says.

She proceeds to smile and then gives a quite long description of the clothes she is wearing, where she bought them, how much they were reduced by. It is in a lot of ways similar to a conversation he might have with a friend about buying a car. The best deal one could get at the best price.

The atmosphere is comfortable in the pub; the pictures of the old town adorn the walls. Dunleavy sits at the bar nursing a half one of whiskey and a stout with no head on it. He talks infrequently to himself. The barmaid flicks TV channels of gardening programmes and soap operas. The conversation is kept carefully away from the subject of work and the very real fact that as far as Miss Kilroy is concerned, Gus has not worked a day in eighteen years, and lives in a filthy caravan in the woods. He has pondered why she agreed to meet him. Is it his rugged good looks? Seeing her now, he begins to think that it is his rebellion which attracts, his haphazard nonconformist attitude to life. Perhaps Miss Kilroy thinks she can change him, she can make him want to work, to get a house and a mortgage, pay a life insurance policy, have children and become chairman of the neighbourhood watch. He does not know if any of that is possible. He does like this woman, likes her smile and her humour, the way she seems to accept his situation. He likes her personality, her self-deprecation once the official mask has been removed.

They walk along the street after closing time. It is a warm still night. August is damp yet humid. She is driving. She says she will drop him home. To his caravan. He pleads he will walk but she insists. He hopes she does not expect him to ask her in. Who knows what lives in that part of the woods at night? He racks his mind to think of some solution as they near the dark forest. She drives adeptly through the road without the hesitation of less than a week ago.

'How do you see your way home, every night?' she asks. He is not often out late, he assures her. Eventually they arrive at the clearing where they first met.

'Well, thanks for a nice evening, Augustus,' she says. They kiss. Her breath smells of vodka. She wears nice perfume. The shampoo smell of her hair surrounds him. He is not at all feeling sexual. He is terrified she will want to come into the caravan. He imagines a convention of hedgehogs waiting at the door.

'Are you around Thursday?' he says.

'Should be,' she replies, tidying herself.

'I'll pick you up at seven,' he says confidently.

'Okay. Are you alright, you look worried about something?'

'Fine,' he says, incredible relief washing over him as he climbs out.

He watches her drive off and quickly runs through the road after her, the red lights of her car a guide in the pitch darkness, until he gets back on the main road and hurries down to the cottage. He doesn't know how to manoeuvre around the problem of the caravan. As much as he is infatuated, he does not want to end up in jail either.

He does not sleep well. He dreams of caravans rolling down hills where he is tied to the road at the bottom. He dreams of giant elephants chasing him around the forest where the caravan is parked. He dreams of Stephen giving him a secondhand suit to wear on his next date.

The ambush of the nurse is initially a tedious operation. He leaves the cottage early on Wednesday morning before either of his parents are up and start becoming frantic about the exposed turf and impending rain. But Miss Needham does not emerge from the clinic all day. He drives up and down the street numerous times. Liam questions him when he buys a Lucozade at one.

'Are you casing somewhere?' he says and laughs. Close enough.

'Testing the brakes in that yoke.'

On Thursday at half twelve, while he is parked near the bridge, Miss Needham emerges. From behind his copy of *The Dealer*, he watches her walk across the road and into The Red Oak. He follows her in a few minutes later. She had seen his car, he was convinced of it. In the end, it is an easy clinch, nice to see you again, oh hello, can I join you, sure, it's a good spot. Today though, the soup is the least edible version of the watery home-made bowl of unwashed celery stumps that Liam usually serves. No comment is made. They talk of work, mainly her work, of farming, of parents, of houses. The one subject they do not discuss is Miss Kilroy. Miss Kilroy is on a distant planet at the moment. Gus is consumed with Miss Needham's blue eyes. He nods attentively as she speaks of the clinic, of her latest transfer, of her family in the east. The conversation turns to the weekend, as it should, and he ventures a supper date on Friday.

It is accepted.

3

Gus shaves with a new razor and takes particular care not to cut himself that evening. The last thing he wants is a piece of newspaper hanging from his chin all the way into town. He chooses a dark shirt which can afford to have the top two buttons opened without looking rakish. He checks his gold chain for any specks of dirt and gives it a rub with a cloth dipped in Brasso.

He feels good as he drives toward the big town where Miss Kilroy lives. It is a semi-detached house on the outskirts. At the door he checks himself again and rings the doorbell. Tanya answers. She wears loose pyjama bottoms. 'Hi, Augustus, come in.'

She shows him to a small sitting room. The footsteps on the stairs raise some excitement and Miss Kilroy enters the room. 'Hello,' she says. They drive off.

They settle on a Chinese restaurant. Gus crunches prawn crackers. His conversation is careful. Miss Kilroy still works for the government. He talks about horses. Women like that type of thing. She tells him there is an equestrian centre near her family home. The conversation has difficulty getting to warmer shores. They have some wine.

He takes her hand as they leave the restaurant. To his surprise, she does not pull it away. Their fingers entwine as they walk down the steps and onto the main street. Gus is warm, he feels good, he feels light. He likes the way her brown eyes seem to float in her face, decorated with loose brown curls. He has her now, he cannot help himself thinking. There is something of great value in the frame of Miss Kilroy, something really worthwhile, he thinks.

They have a drink in The Postman. She is saying something about her job, her supervisor. He is a bully, she says. She didn't want to work in the civil service, she used to paint,

paint landscapes. But that kind of work is frowned upon where she comes from. Bohemian. State jobs are secure. Gus nods. He tries to listen but is distracted. There are other more pressing matters.

'Are you going to come in for a coffee?' she asks, outside the house.

'Oh, yeah, I will,' he says, wondering about that.

They enter, it is silent, Tanya is out. They sit in the kitchen at the table close together. She makes him a fancy sounding coffee with a percolator. It tastes rich. He is nervous, he feels like his tongue is hanging out.

'Very nice coffee.'

'Yeah? Nicer than your brew at the caravan?'

They laugh in step. He realises she does not believe he lives in the caravan, she never believed it. Was going through the motions, just like he was. A vulnerability seems to emerge in her face, somewhere around her eyes.

'That was my best jar,' he protests. She smiles deeply, without reservation of any kind, she will let him kiss her, kiss her properly, he senses. He goes for it. She responds, her tongue touches his. He feels very warm. He feels bizarrely awkward as they break off and the walk to the bedroom awaits. She takes his hand and romantically they walk through the little hall, and up the stairs. They sit on the bed and continue to kiss. In the bedroom, as her hand arrives on his chest, he lets go of his nerves and relaxes, enjoying her touch, beginning to roam around her body, helping her undress and she does the same to him. They get under the sheets, naked skin on skin, warm, close, feeling good, feeling very good.

He often worries about his performance in these situations but she seems content enough, she seems satisfied, afterwards, she puts her palm on his chest and cuddles close to him.

'I enjoyed tonight,' she says.

'So did I,' Gus says, thinking about a plate of sausages.

'You can sleep for a while, I have to get up at seven,' she says, as he drifts off.

'Okay,' he mumbles.

When he awakes, she is gone. The house is quiet. His parents will be asking a hundred questions. He will bring some bacon home with him, he decides, it will smooth the reception. The last thing he feels like now is the clucking of two pensioners, with the smell of Miss Kilroy still on him. He will not shower until later, he thinks. He goes into the bathroom and tosses some water on himself.

The car is cold. The night before is like a great film he watched. He relives every scene, every word of dialogue. There is something he really liked about Miss Kilroy. Is she flawed like him, he wonders? After the inevitable Q & A session at the cottage, he gets up on the half-stripped roof and lies at an angle thinking about Miss Kilroy. Thinking about her body.

'What are you at?' his father yells from below.

'Measuring something, go inside will ya, it's gone cold.'

Miss Kilroy sends him a text. 'Hi. Drink this evening?'

'Bingo with mother. Sorry. Tomorrow at five?' he replies.

A smiley is the response.

In the Country Kitchen restaurant that evening, he eats a plate of lasagne and chips. Miss Needham has a salad. She talks about pensioners, sick people. The city. Her blue eyes instantly remove the lingering taste of Miss Kilroy. They drive around the lake afterwards. There is a full moon. It shines a pale bar along the top of the water.

'It's a lovely place here,' she says. The problem is the people, not the place, he thinks.

Her rented house is bigger than Miss Kilroy's. The carpet is worn. There are scribble marks on the walls. The relics of a family who have separated and are living in distant places, in distant lives. Miss Needham is hopeful of a permanent job in the surgery, he hears. Other details drift over his head, like lost swirling dust particles. On the sofa they kiss, she tastes different, feels different. In her room there are numerous cosmetics, a large alarm clock, a diary, a wardrobe of endless clothes and a small guitar in the corner.

'You play?' he asks, as they sit on the bed.

'Sometimes, a little. When I've time.'

Miss Needham is fairer than Miss Kilroy, but not better-looking. Her body is no less taut, no less warm. She reacts to his movements in other ways, at other times. Her breath has a slightly mintier air about it.

The next day he has a raging headache. In the kitchen, he tells them he cannot do anything on the roof, he is dizzy. He tries to do the crossword at the kitchen table. His father watches a programme about trout fishing. His mother cleans the cooker.

His headache clears by evening. Miss Kilroy wears a leather trouser and kisses him when they meet. She looks even prettier than he remembers. They speak of yesterday. He talks of the galvanise roof and his father's commentary on his work. She laughs about that. She says she was very busy, a lot of people looking for heating allowance that she finds have sheds full of turf. System is wrong, she says. Aye, he agrees with that. She tells him she put a note on his file to hurry up his claim. He thanks her. They make love in her flat.

Gus feels happy as he urinates at home that night. He wonders about the future. It is not his fault. How was he to know both Marys would be so accommodating to his charms? It had never happened before. Was he expected to meekly walk away?

He demands his conscience to defend the isolation in the bog, the lack of company, the loneliness, the constant loneliness. And then simply discard potential contentment? No, there will have to be a slow let down on one side. But he cannot decide on which side as of yet. It will happen of its own accord. For the moment it will continue in the vein it has. The blonde and the brunette. Weaved together in his dreams. At the moment it is like a pint of stout, mixed, swirling, toward the lip of the glass. All at sea, all twisting and turning in his head, toing and froing, he does not know which way to turn and does not want to turn either way. But some day the pint will settle and a clear line will divide black and white.

The sun shines again on Sunday morning. Gus stands at the back of the church as usual. At the end of one pew he sees Frank Deane is home. His face tanned from the Las Vegas sun. He looks out and the silver Mercedes is parked at the church door. He looks back, Deane has caught his eye. Deane smiles broadly, winking, even giving him a quick thumbs-up. A pang of irritation rises in him. Pleb. His mobile purrs in his pocket from text messages. He knows they are either from Miss Needham or Miss Kilroy. He takes out the phone. Miss Kilroy wants to go to the beach. Miss Needham wants to go to a forest park. He decides on the beach. He tells Miss Needham he has to help his father with some shelves for the afternoon but he will be free this evening. He will be finished with Miss Kilroy by then. The priest discusses forgiveness.

Outside, there is a collection. Gus has mastered the art of avoiding church gate collections quite well. He parks far away and will walk through the gap in the fence. He will not pass the collection. There is a certain fear that he will make some remark about why he should support whatever charity it is. Is he not enough of a charity, he would like to ask them. Franny Morrin blocks his way, he talks to Gus about wooden stakes for twenty minutes. By the time Gus has escaped, most people have left the church yard, including the collectors. Even the priest is out, now dressed in his black clothes. 'Hello Father,' Gus says.

'Gus. Are you up to your old tricks?' the priest says, smiling.

Gus does not like this comment, but he smiles and the priest walks on. What did he mean by that, Gus wonders? Is he not a good Christian, minding his parents in the winter of their lives? He didn't even get the land.

His mother is putting a pot of potatoes on the range when he arrives home. The smell of burning lamb is in the kitchen. His father coughs as he enters.

'Have you got no syrup?' Gus says. It is hard to listen to the bubbling of mucus in his father's throat. He takes out the *Sunday World* and sits on his comfortable armchair. Somewhere in the sports pages, he remembers the invite to the beach. He takes out the phone. He types: 'Yes, 2. Have to be back for cards at 6.' Keep a curfew. Do not want to be too late. There has to be a limit. Women who think they can call you at their pleasure become complacent. It is only one more step to talk of settling down. Love and marriage. This is dangerous territory and it must be carefully negotiated.

The road is sticking to the wheels as they drive to the west and the sea, the golden sand and blue skies. It is like a different country.

'A great country when the weather is right,' Gus says. Miss Kilroy does not respond. Her silence like that worries him. It is as though he is losing her somehow, losing control. He has to be careful. It is a fine art. Too much control, they feel trapped. Not enough control, they feel you do not care. It is a skill, a nod, a word, a grunt at the right moment. A language to itself.

The beach is busy. Families with all sorts of contraptions. Deckchairs. Towel racks. Umbrellas. Portable fridges. Somebody has a barbecue and is frying sausages. Gus wants to sit in the car, looking at the ocean, but she wants to walk in the sand. She takes off her sandals and lets the sand in her feet. She tells him to do the same but he refuses. A thought crosses his mind as they walk along holding hands. The possibility of Miss Needham deciding to go to the beach. He looks around, his heart beating. It had not occurred to him before. There is no one there he recognises. Unlikely to see any of the villagers out sunning themselves.

Blondes rubbing suntan lotion into their slender arms. He looks across the sea to the peninsula, up the coast. He and McCluskey will be up there soon. There is something attractive about it right at that moment. Safer. They talk about her job. She is thinking of getting a transfer. The workload is too high.

They get an ice-cream and a cappuccino in the ice-cream parlour when they are leaving. He likes ice-cream. Cool against the heat of the sun. He likes the rig-out Miss Kilroy is wearing; he had been distracted and only noticed it now. He feels himself getting aroused. This could be tricky. This will be tricky. He decides not to allude to it at all. They drive back towards the town. No arrangements for sex have been mentioned. She eventually asks him in for a coffee. He never drinks any coffee. Afterwards it is half five. He dresses hurriedly and pecks her on the cheek. He senses that she is not happy but there is nothing he can do. There is more work to be done.

Miss Needham is dressed in a splendid dark navy ensemble. She has a nice royal blue purse to go with it. Really, she is too well dressed for The Red Oak. Reilly speaks animatedly alone in the corner. There are three large-bellied figures at the other end of the counter who have done the day since Mass. Their conversation has degenerated into idle murmurings to each other which none of them understand. Miss Needham has long thin arms which he wants to runs his hand along slowly. It is fun to talk with her, to bring her back to her place, to feel her body, to see her long blonde hair fall around the side of her naked chest, for his eyes, for his eyes only.

The great thing about Miss Needham is that she does not know he is officially unemployed. That is a sticking point for Miss Kilroy. He can guess it in her eyes, at the beach it was in her mind, what future with this guy? Whereas he has implied, very covertly, that he will give the farm which he does not own to Miss Needham. There may be more possibilities there. Not in words, of course, never in words. She is visiting her family in the city next weekend, she is saying. He could come if he likes. Awkward. A full weekend away from Miss Kilroy. He says he will see.

When she is asleep, he ponders things. Still no word from McCluskey. His dole money is very small. Petrol for his car does not be too long drinking it. A nice top or a pair of shoes does for the rest. It is alright for Stephen with the big farm of land. It is alright for his sister in England married to rich Ron, the stock trader's son.

By one the next day he has most of the sheets off the roof. He develops a prising system which destabilises the iron grip the rusted screws have on the timber. He finds an old can of creosote in the boot of his Lancer and after some difficulties opening the lid, he begins painting it onto the old rafters. His father coughs and spits from the door, observing the process with undisguised disgust.

'The smell of that stuff,' he says, patting the seat of his pants as he turns back into the house. Gus makes some progress the following days. He removes the rest of the sheets. One rafter is rotten through and he pulls it off with the old stabilising bar. He will have to go to the coastal town and buy a length of six by two.

There are a few texts, a few calls from the two Marys. He handles them well. 'Busy. See you the weekend.' Smiley face added. He extends his poem. 'The Official and the Nurse,' he writes on Wednesday evening. Later he thinks it is not very poetic. He is disappointed.

On Thursday, he gets up at eight before his mother starts demanding turf at the range. He showers in the little bathroom and looks at himself in the mirror as he dries off. He notices his belly has started to sag over his pelvic area. Some diet, he thinks, his red hair standing on the back of his neck. He has stopped taking milk in his tea, stopped eating bread, potatoes and yoghurt and all that has happened is his belly has sank. He decides he will write a poem about this. He sits on the toilet bowl with his notebook. 'The Belly,' it will be called. He puts the biro on the page. No words come. He decides to think about it for a while. He dabs his jaw with aftershave.

He gets to the little market town on the coast. At Maloney's he collects a length of nine by two and, with it tied on the roof, he decides to take his time coming home. He likes to be alone sometimes for a few hours. It is a break from his parents, from Miss Kilroy and Miss Needham, from the galvanise roof, from wondering if McCluskey will ring. It had been difficult to arrange the trip to the city with Miss Needham and explain to Miss Kilroy his complete absence for the weekend. A fishing trip in the south with Franny Morrin is the choice he made.

He walks along the path, noticing tourists with maps, pensioners with rosary beads, children on school holidays playing catch. He stops for no real reason and looks at the river flowing beneath the bridge. The water relentlessly tosses and dances along. It is not very deep; he can see the worn pebbles beneath. He imagines stripping naked and jumping in, lying down on those pebbles and drifting away into a deep, dark sleep.

He looks across at birds gathering in the tree branches. He supposes preparing for the winter migration. He wouldn't mind a migration for the winter. Somewhere faraway. A different country. But no. He has never travelled. He probably never will. He takes out his notebook and looks at his scrawled handwriting. 'The Belly'. The idea seems stupid now. He thinks it should be about the river below him. 'Flowing.' He likes 'Flowing'. He writes 'Flowing' down. He puts the notebook on the stone wall at the road and writes it. 'Flowing. The river flows.' He writes: 'The river flows'. 'The river flows along', like, like, he looks at the sky, 'Like a cloud.' 'The river flows along like a cloud.' Terrible.

He goes to The Port, the pub on the corner. He orders a pot of tea and a scone. He decides he will do twenty sit-ups every morning. That might remove the bulge. A drunken man comes into the pub.

'Pint of stout! Great day...' the man says to the wall. 'Yeah, yeah, yeah, yeah'.

Gus finishes his tea quickly and leaves.

At home, he sits in the kitchen listening to the farm news. Cattle are up. Of course they should have sold their cattle this month. He is the farmer here by rights. He should have got the farm. The others were better educated, they had careers. He was the one that needed help. The incident in the peninsula aside, he really should have got the farm. He cannot sleep that night.

On Friday, the scent of autumn is in the air. The year is changing, a chill is present that was not there before. In the yard, he looks up at the roof. The length of nine by two lies idly in the yard awaiting its positioning amongst the other rafters. But he does not feel like doing that job today. There are many jobs like that. Easy to start. Very difficult to finish. There is the garden wall he started a few years ago. The concrete path at the front. The half-built doghouse. The half fixed-up old Morris Minor his grandfather once drove. Half-jobs. Halfway. He is a halfway man, he thinks. Maybe he could change the oil in the Lancer. Something about the mechanisation of the job excites him. He goes into the village and buys a filter at Niland's garage. He returns home and with a screwdriver, removes the old filter. Drains the oil from the engine, replaces the sump plug, puts in the new oil.

'It's no length since you changed that,' his father shouts from the back door as he sniffs a handkerchief and coughs deeply.

'Much you know about it,' Gus mutters.

The oil leaves a small dark stain on the gravel. The rain will get that, he thinks. It will eventually cut through the grease, through a mixture of erosion and persistence. No texts or calls from any of the women since Wednesday. He was due to hit the road for the city at five with Miss Needham. Meet the folks. Crackers.

When he returns inside for tea, there is a message. There was a phone call earlier. The apartments at Killabilloo are ready. McCluskey is going back to work on Monday. Killabilloo. The smallest backward hole in the county. At the top of the peninsula, not where the fracas happened but still in that general area. He will be moving there for the week. It may go on longer; there may be more than one apartment ready. But even a week would be a long time to be gone from his parents.

On Friday evening Gus collects Miss Needham, 'In The Mood' playing on low. They set off for the city. She wears flame-shaped dangling earrings and a turquoise blouse. Her perfume lifts him to another dimension.

The land flattens out as he drives through the midlands. Sprawling housing estates have mushroomed amongst abandoned bogs. On large signs regularly planted along the dual carriageway, giant smiling people happily hold the keys to their new homes.

Mrs. Needham is a sprightly woman in her fifties. Gus sees some likeness. The same blue eyes with a less energetic flicker to them. She provides tea on a china cup and saucer. Gus has difficulty putting his finger and thumb around the cup handle.

'And what do you do, yourself, Augustus?' Miss Needham's mother says.

'Farming,' Gus says. Landed would be the word used around here, Gus imagines. The landed gentry.

'Well done,' Mrs. Needham says, in the tone one comments on a five-year-old's drawing. They go to the cinema. It is a film about a man who inherits many millions but must spend it all in a month. A remake. Gus has little trouble absorbing himself in the fantasy. They make love in her small bed.

The journey back seems long. Miss Needham appears to be in love with someone. Gus is hoping it is not him. She is gushing with chat and talk about this and that, things he could never in his wildest imagination have considered, things like the strap on a heel, the tightness of a blouse, the heat and the cold. She even wants to meet his parents.

It is a relief to get back to the thatched house on Sunday evening.

4

Early next morning, the van trundles along at a legal and respectable thirty-five miles an hour. McCluskey's mug, the cold tea bag stuck to the side near the rim, rattles above the blaring radio. The van struggles as it tackles the inclines toward the higher altitude of the north of the county.

'It's time you changed this yoke,' Gus blurts.

'What's wrong with ya?' McCluskey sneers.

It is Gus' usual tricky humour the first day back at work. This was going to be a particularly straining experience. A week working in a distant village in the north of the county. The most pressing issue was the collection of Gus' weekly welfare payment.

'Can you get them to transfer it?' McCluskey says, his owl eyes widening.

'No, I cannot. I'll have to go down and collect it.'

'Well, I don't know can we allow that,' McCluskey says.

'You'll just have to allow it.'

A text message. 'Hi. How are you?'

'Mary' was the sender. Aye. He thought of her body.

The site is silent until half eight when other trades arrive: carpenters, looking tired and bored; plumbers; electricians in a white van. A few blocklayers set up near half-built garden walls. Larry the foreman arrives within a huge Land Rover. Although a new model, the vehicle is spattered with hardened cement and thick wads of dried mud around the crevices of the body, giving it a somewhat veteran look. The dash is full of receipts.

'So lads, how are things down the glen?' says Larry, at the first tea break.

'Same as ever,' McCluskey responds, his huge mouth devouring an enormous salmon sandwich.

'That woman looks after you well,' Freddy, the bony site labourer says. He stares into McCluskey's lunchbox.

'Well, you must understand,' McCluskey says, adopting his occasional highly informed tone, 'If you treat the little woman right, they will treat you right.'

'And how do you do that?' Freddy says. He leans on a shovel as he munches a Snickers.

'Keep her in silver,' McCluskey says. 'But not too much.'

The group absorb this piece of wisdom. Gus mulls over his poem as he eats a ham sandwich. 'Beautiful trees, beautiful flowers. Lakes and Mountains all around.'

Once the first tea break is over the day moves quickly. They skim coat all the ceilings in the flat. The evening is spent attaching aluminium bead at the frames around the inside of the windows.

'This window board isn't level, where did he get these fellas?' McCluskey says, as Gus washes out buckets.

'Nothing is level around here, including the locals,' Gus replies, emptying drops of water from the former tile grout container.

Another text message: 'Fancy coming north on Saturday? I've an evening wedding invite, Mary.' More visits to families. He is still getting over the trip to Dublin. Already Miss Needham wants to meet his mother and it won't be long before the other one follows suit. Bananas. Maybe he is better off in Killabilloo.

They arrive at Hattigan's little cottage at half six. Hattigan makes a big thing of welcoming the two, as though they had arrived at the biggest hotel in Europe. He carries in their two bags with the efficiency of a bell-boy. However, his wellingtons, Guns n' Roses cap and loose jeans spoil the effect somewhat.

'Not bad,' McCluskey says across the hall, as they settle into each room.

'What is he charging?' Gus asks.

'Sssshh. Lord almighty, don't mention that in the house, jaysus.'

'What?'

'You can't say anything about money,'

'Are you not giving him anything?'

'Sure what is it costing him?'

'He's renting rooms, you tight c–'

'Be quiet! Let's get the dinner…'

They go to the hotel on the village's sole street. Killabilloo has an abandoned atmosphere. The only thing missing, Gus thinks, is a ball of dust rolling across the road. The hotel is quiet, even though it is the last week of August.

'Gentlemen,' the man behind the bar says, a thin grey-haired man of late forties. He wears a pair of glasses and an attentive air.

'Two beers,' McCluskey says. 'Do you do grub?'

'We do indeed,' the manager says, handing them two menus.

There are two others at the counter. One drinks pint glasses of Ribena. He tells them he is off the drink twenty years but likes the company. Another, a massively overweight red-haired man, announces to the contingent that he has been hawking lentils over window frames all day as he swallows pint after pint. 'Not a single block laid today, not one. They don't see all that when they're yapping about the great money per block we get…'.

There is a general murmur of agreement. There is a kind of solidarity here, Gus thinks, the great persecuted re-group after a day of offering their services to the others: the contractors, the owners, the developers. The beer tastes slightly stale. Gus looks at the television: the new football season has just begun. He is just getting interested in the game when his phone rings. He walks out to the toilet lobby. 'Hello?'

'Don't answer texts, do you not?'

'How are you, Mary? Yeah...everything is going well here...no bother...what time does the ferry leave at?' In the absence of any other alternative, he agrees to the journey north.

The manager, whose name is confirmed as being Peter by his regular clientele, brings out the meals: roast beef, potatoes, carrots, peas, gravy, Yorkshire pudding.

'Looks good,' McCluskey says, unrolling the cutlery from the dainty handkerchief, lost amongst his thick fingers. He snorts and begins devouring; his elbows on the counter as he dishes the food back at pace.

'Will you take your time?' Gus says. He tentatively sprinkles his food with salt.

'You know, that would be an insult if ye were in France,' the fat block layer says.

'Why is that?' Gus replies.

'The chef seasons the food, not the customer.'

'I thought the customer was always right.'

'Yeah, but he's meant to taste the food as the chef seasoned it, and then put the salt as much as he wants. You haven't even tasted that and you're dousing it in salt.'

'Hmm.' Gus looks at the steaming food in front of him. He was not expecting restaurant etiquette lessons in Killabilloo. He looks to his right. McCluskey wipes his plate with a piece of bread. He finishes his pint of beer and starts making a rolly.

'Jeez Pat, you should go to the Olympics. That's just piggery.'

'What's wrong with ya?' the owl-eyed one retorts.

'How long are ye down for?' Peter inquires. Good way of putting it, Gus thinks. Down in the cusp of a nightmare, deep in the bog. The autumn wind outside is beginning to pick up. Gus notices the petrol station's ice-cream cone figure is shaking in the breeze.

'A few weeks.'

'A week,' Gus corrects his employer.

'Well,' McCluskey looks at Peter. 'We don't know, it depends on the fellas ahead of us, chippies and whatnot.'

'Hmm,' Gus interjects.

'Dessert?' Peter says, as he takes McCluskey's place.

'No thanks.' McCluskey leaves no doubt hanging in the air on that subject. 'One for the road and we'll be off.'

Gus' bed is uncomfortable and Hattigan's house is very near the road. For such an isolated place there is a lot of traffic passing at eleven. On their way for a late pint, he thinks. There is nothing around the countryside here, only owls hooting and car lights. He gets up at two and urinates. He wanders around the house and goes out through the kitchen, Hattigan's battered old fridge humming in the darkness. He goes outside, feels the cool night air in his lungs, on his bare legs. The cold path on his feet. He walks along, enjoying the different blue world he is in. Hattigan has a panoramic view of the bay at the back of his house. The surface is perfectly still. Gus stares out into the night for a long time.

It is September 1st. Hattigan munches toast at half seven. Gus is woken by the smell of burning tobacco from McCluskey's room. Gus feels he is sleepwalking as he tries to eat his cornflakes. It was one thing yesterday morning coming from his own bed, but here he feels like he didn't sleep at all, twisting and turning all night in a restless stupor. Even the tea tastes different. Hattigan is watching a small portable TV on top of the fridge. A politician is speaking. The sound is muted.

'Bastards,' Hattigan is saying, 'They're all bastards...'

'Oh they are,' McCluskey says, his huge mouth swallowing three slices of bread together.

'Never did a day's work in their lives.'

'Oh, that's it.'

'What's wrong with your man?' Hattigan says, nodding toward Gus, who holds his mug in suspended animation, while staring pensively out the window.

'Oh, he's always like that, our buck. Bit of a dreamer.'

'You mind yourself,' Gus retorts, getting up and leaving the kitchen.

'In a mood I'd say. All these women he has going on.' McCluskey says in a mumble.

'What was that?' Gus says, looking back from the long hall. His eyes pierce from the hall darkness, like a cat on a night time motorway.

'Nawthin', nawthin'.'

The drive to the site takes five minutes. Gus yawns as the day comes into focus. McCluskey drains a chipped cup he has requisitioned from Hattigan's scattered kitchen and sucks hungrily on a crooked roll-up.

'I'm floating upstairs,' McCluskey says, as he gets out.

'And where's the other man?'

'What other man?'

'The other man that's going to help me carry buckets upstairs all day?'

'Hahaha!' McCluskey laughs and walks off.

Gus feels himself getting hotter. His red hair is beginning to scratch him. He hadn't shaved this morning, he realises. He starts the mixer after some efforts. It is one of the old types that require a Herculean effort to swing. He spends at least fifteen minutes getting organised and can hear McCluskey scratching his mortar board upstairs impatiently. Gus knows the plasterer becomes more and more agitated as minutes tick by without walls being coated and notes being earned.

The threshold has a piece of timber across it to help the barrow up. When the wheel of the barrow passes the door threshold, it weighs the timber down on the inside. The other end lifts and strikes Gus on the shin. He roars to the air. The phone beeps with a message. He stops in the hall, rubbing his stinging leg and looks for his phone amongst the deep camouflage trouser he wears to work.

'Muck, muck, muck!' McCluskey shouts, with the same tone he uses for cattle when he arrives with a bag of meal in the autumn fields, using the words 'Chuff, chuff, chuff!' in that scenario.

'Hi, free tomorrow night?' Miss Needham. Unlikely. He will probably be here in the dark with his ample-posteriored employer. He fills the buckets with mortar and climbs the steps. A day of this repetition stretches out before him. He could have been a poet. He could have been an *actore*.

'What were you at? Christ, I've half an hour lost already...' McCluskey says, as Gus arrives with two buckets. Gus tosses the mortar out.

'That mix is a bit heavy,' McCluskey says, sweeping a hawkful. He starts coating the nearest wall.

'You know I have to go home to collect money tomorrow.'

'Uh? I don't know about this type of criminal activity.'

'How else would you get away with these wages?'

'Ha ha. Yeah, yeah. I suppose. We'll go up and down after the tea.'

Ugh. No escape. He goes back downstairs and fills another two buckets. His heart is just not in it today. Another message. What is it this time? He is hungry. He wishes it was ten o'clock.

'What time will you be ready on Saturday? Do you have a white shirt? Mary xx.' That would be Miss Kilroy. He thinks. Mother of God. White shirts. Pure Madness.

'Muck, muck, muck!' McCluskey shouts. Gus can't even think of a response. The next hour goes slowly. With a flat plastic tool, McCluskey begins to smooth off the sand and cement he has coated the walls with. They move into the master bedroom. This takes a lot of mixes. Gus gets tired. It is getting near one o'clock and the second break. Gus feels a pang of hunger and gets another message from Miss Kilroy.

'Are you not talking to me?'

'Muck, muck, muck!'

'Have you your phone on?' Miss Needham.

'Muck, muck, muck!'

'Stop that!' Gus roars at the bedroom.

'What?'

'Stop saying that!'

'What?'

'Talking to me like I'm one of your suck calves, who do you think you are, anyway?'

'Arragh, if you don't like it, why are you here?'

'Well, I don't like it, if it's anything to ya.'

'Well, go so.'

'Well, I will so.'

'Will you tell Larry to send Freddy up?' McCluskey shouts out the window as Gus reaches the site gate.

Gus walks the two miles back to Hattigans. For some minutes, the anger resounds through him, the chant 'Muck, muck, muck!' still ringing in his ears. But soon, he is shrouded in a great sense of freedom, he feels like he is mitching school again, almost sheepish as cars pass him, the drivers waving. He imagines their thoughts: Who is that? Who is this character, I wonder?

It is 2 o'clock when he gets back to the house. Hattigan is asleep, his head sideways on the kitchen table. His dog looks nervously out the window. The shopping channel is on the silent TV. Gus grabs his bag.

The road is quiet at lunchtime on a Wednesday. Gus repeatedly walks around in a slow circle.

Some hours later, Gus arrives back at the cottage having travelled through the contributory efforts of a curious couple from Killabilloo, a depressed sales agent and a Texan tourist who had just retired and was living his dream in a light blue Volkswagen Camper van.

He spends the evening absent-mindedly lying across a rusting sheet on the turf shed roof. His parents repeatedly question him about his unexpected return, questions which he ignores. His phone has fifteen messages on it. There are ten missed calls. He lights a cigarette and sits back. He smokes two or three cigarettes every month. He does not know why, he just does.

Late at night, he works on his poem in the bedroom. 'Mountains, clouds and trees in the sky'. 'Grass flows in the breeze.' He writes this down hurriedly and reads it as though the words might disappear.

In the morning he collects his dole payment at the post office beside The Red Oak. He drives back to the job. In one of the small bedrooms, McCluskey is putting up beads.

'Oh you came back, did you?'

They do some skimming. Gus runs a trowel along the hardening skimcoat as McCluskey flattens it out. There is an echo now in the skimmed rooms.

'You would a been good spread in your day,' McCluskey remarks.

'Wouldn't lower myself.'

'Ha ha.' Gus gathers up the old skim bags and carries them outside. He puts a small drop of petrol on them, cautiously watching the flat for any sign of a pair of thrifty owl-eyes. He finds a lighter and after some efforts in the Atlantic breeze, smoke begins to filter out from the pile in a dry corner of the site. He watches the plastic inner wrapping curl up, enjoying the smell of burning paper.

In the evening, Peter smiles as they enter the hotel bar.

'How are ye lads?' he says, efficiently plucking two cardboard menus from somewhere and placing on the counter. The block layer is swilling away. The Ribena addict sits at the corner playing with a beer mat. Gus imagines standing up in the middle of the bar, taking out his notebook and reading his poem. 'Beautiful mountain, distant trees. Lost flowers, busy bees.' Nobody had ever heard his poetry. Nobody knows he writes poetry. If it is poetry. Maybe it is nothing.

As they eat, Peter talks about buying a new car. 'I think I might try one. You know, you see people with all these lovely new motors and you're working away and you've a pile of shit. Goes the same for women.' He looks cautiously around. 'You know what I mean, lads? You're married to the same woman for twenty, ah, twenty-five years. It gets to you. You see all these, you know. You know, these…' he makes an hourglass figure sign with his hands, 'and you think mmm. Mmm. Ketchup, butter?'

He places a condiment holder in front of McCluskey, even though the plasterer is already wiping his plate clean.

'What do you think, Pat? Ever consider trading up?

'As I always say,' McCluskey slips out a Rizla paper efficiently with thumb and forefinger as he speaks. 'It doesn't matter where a man gets his appetite as long as he has the dinner at home.'

'There doesn't look to be much wrong with your appetite for anything anyway,' Gus says, staring at McCluskey's plate as he reaches for the ketchup.

A family arrive at the door. Peter beckons them in.

Gus observes the unit they present. It makes him feel uneasy. He feels tenseness around his neck and a terror that something is going to roar at him any moment. Both Miss Kilroy and Miss Needham will want families. Their child-bearing hips are in perfect order, oh yes, he can testify to that, it would be a shame not to reproduce. They are like prime heifers not being bulled.

As they sit at the bar munching the fresh food, Peter whispers to Gus. 'That's the boss in.'

'Really, is he the owner?'

'He bought this place a couple of years ago. One of these hot shot accountants, you know. Building an empire. Married into The Low Chaparral in Barhill. This old place is just another leg in his portfolio, you know yourself–'

'The Low Chaparral?'

Gus looks around. It is indeed Sandra, fifteen years on, sitting with the three children while a man sits beside her, scanning a laptop. Gus carefully shields his face and turns back toward the bar.

After another hoovering of his plate, McCluskey announces he will go back to Hattigans for a sleep. He will come down later for a couple, to kill off the rest of the night. Gus follows McCluskey out and decides to take a walk around the village. The day is drawing to a close but there is still some light. Some crows stare at him from a telegraph line. He takes out his notebook and writes, 'Two sparrows.' No. 'Two butterflies. Flapping in the wind. The man tries to catch them with his net. He catches two. Which does he keep or does he keep both? No, he cannot keep both, only one. But which one?' It is not really a poem, he thinks. He does a circle of the village and arrives back at the hotel. He stands at a corner and watches Sandra and her family leave. The children are crying over the lack of ice-cream. Gus feels a headache coming on.

He does not sleep well. The nights in Hattigan's room are long and boring. He tires of the banter between McCluskey and the foreman on the site. He tires of talking football with Freddy. He wants to get out of this place. They will be leaving Friday. The sooner, the better.

On Thursday, Miss Needham calls. She does not seem too pleased. Wanting to know would he ever be around again. What sort of relationship was it, anyway? If he was just messing, he could mess somewhere else. It is difficult to conduct this conversation while carrying in bags of skim coat plaster from a pick-up truck driven by a man in a fierce hurry. But he uses every ounce of persuasion he can. He tells her he would bring her out on Saturday. She wants to know where. Wait and see, he tells her. A surprise. He would think of something. The conversation ended on a better note.

'That's it for a week or so. I hope them ludramons get the next one ready by Monday week. If they haven't, I've a massive bungalow down south that I can probably do,' McCluskey says, as they load his tools back into the van on Friday afternoon.

'No panic. I've my roof to finish off,' Gus says, folding his wages into his pocket.

'You should have got Twomey.'

'Arragh, that fella would rob ya. It's surprising what one man can do over a few weeks.'

5

When Gus gets home his father is coughing and spluttering.

'He's on antibiotics but they don't seem to do him any good,' his mother says. Gus looks at his father closely. Old man Watt seems to have shrunk during the week. A shrivelled shell of a man now. Barely able to speak, let alone criticise whatever it is he feels Gus is doing wrong, he estimates. Gus puts his working clothes into the washing machine.

'Ughuh! You'll have it blocked with all that bleddy cement. Ughuh!' He's not dead yet.

Later, Gus calls Gerry 'Boggo' Kilboggan to arrange a day out for Miss Needham. He hadn't seen the former local pet-neuterer for some months but there was a rumour Boggo was now administering a local whiskey distillery, it might be different and interesting. It was said he was making 'colossal' money selling his produce to the islanders, who certainly didn't 'give a hoot' about excise duty anomalies and whatnot. He imagines a large warehouse beside Boggo's house, lines of fermenting glass flasks and siphons bubbling, perhaps Boggo in a neat distillery uniform, standing in an aisle, examining a clear tube of local produce. Probably this was unrealistic. Yet it should be stimulating and ease the sharpness of his later departure. At first, Boggo does not answer the phone. He tries again.

'Hullo?' There is loud music in the background.
'Are you okay for me to call tomorrow? I've a visitor.'
'Huh?'
'I was thinking around two?'
'Two? Two in the day?'
'Are ya aright, Boggo?'
'Who is this?'

'It's me, Gus.'

'Oh. When you get here, let me know, will ya?'

Gus considers this. 'Okay.'

He gets Miss Kilroy on the phone. She seems in good form. They will leave for the island at five. There should be enough time to show Miss Needham around the distillery and dispatch her. The mass-and-mother excuse will have to be utilised once more. Saturday night is constantly problematic, both demand his presence. Soon the decision will have to be made, to abandon one of the Marys. But not yet. He cannot do that yet.

Next morning, Gus picks up twenty galvanise sheets from Maloney's.

'Them sheets won't take paint,' his father, apparently somewhat recovered, announces from the kitchen window as Gus struggles with reversing the little trailer into the back yard.

'They're dipped, they don't need paint, will you close that window?'

When he calls for Miss Needham, she is wearing a white jeans and striped top. Her blonde hair dangles down around her shoulder.

'Hey,' he says, as she gets in. 'Just Friends' plays low.

'Hi. So where are we going?'

'A mystery tour.'

Boggo's small house is accessed by a winding boreen bordered by wild gorse bushes in the midst of sparse fields. Terrain becomes boggier as they reach the base of the mountain behind. Here, he had once attempted to have the council support a cable-car scheme which he imagined would create instant wealth through eager tourists.

There is no pristine newly-established manufacturing warehouse. Boggo's yard is scattered with bottles and jars, pipes and potato skins. Grass grows all over the once proud path to the front door. There is no drive to speak of, just a sprawling mass of weeds over gravel. They get out and look around.

'Could use a woman's touch,' Miss Needham says.

'Could use a bulldozer,' Gus says with a grunt, looking in the windows.

The glass is thick with dust; he can only make out vague shapes, none of which are moving. He raps the glass.

'Hey, Boggo? Bogs? Hello?'
A text message arrives.

'Aren't you going to check that?'

'The old lady probably wanting me to bring back bananas. Gerry?'

A small window is pushed open. Boggo looks out, his face thick with sweat, his eyes bleary.

'Hu-hag...'

'What are you at? Why don't you open the door?'

'Hu-hu…'

His head disappears within. Gus wants to say arragh, we'll leave it, let's go to the beach. But she will be concerned now. Boggo looked half-dead. Like he needed a hospital bed. He tries to open the back door. 'Open the door will ya?'

Gus checks the text message. 'Bring your swimming gear. There is a pool at the hotel. M xx.'

'Ah! The old lady. Bananas and ham. Might have guessed.' Gus says.

He eventually pushes in the door. Inside bottles line every shelf and press. The house looks like a laboratory after an earthquake. Tubes and rusty weighing scales. Potatoes lie scattered amongst the debris. The table holds three open bags of flour, the powder spilling out onto the raw timber counter. A relic of the cottage's former glow lies against one wall, a tall sideboard. Behind the dusty glass panels hang long untouched china cups.

Flies buzz around, dying as the winter approaches. It is easier to see out the windows than in, but only marginally.

Boggo sits sweating in a faded armchair. He is shaking uncontrollably. He lifts a weak hand and points at a pile of potatoes, and then a large gallon drum. It is half-full of a clear liquid.

Did you have to do that in front of her, Gus thinks. He was just going to say something like, 'Is the heart giving you trouble again?' He doesn't know whether this experience has helped matters with Miss Needham. He cannot say from her outward appearance.

They spend the afternoon walking around the foot of the mountain. The air is clear out here; anything is a relief from Boggo's 'factory'.

'He is an alcoholic, that man,' she says. There is a hint of clinical tone in the statement.

'Well, he probably overdid it this time,' Gus says.

'That stuff he was drinking. Homemade.'

'Yeah. It was surely. I don't know, I thought…you'd like to see the operation.'

'Not after seeing the effects, not really.'

'Oh.'

He suddenly gets an idea for a poem as he looks up at the hill. 'Hill of Earth, speak to me, speak to me like you have never spoken, guide me what to do with this…this gift of nature.'

'He lives on his own there,' Gus declares.

'I could see that.'

The departure from Miss Needham is less than satisfactory, although she masks her displeasure quite well. Helpless, he drives to the county town and sets off north with Miss Kilroy, onto a new link road and on for two hours, through the northern hills and valleys until they reach the windy port and the ferry to her island. The wind is stronger off the mainland tossing the ferry around in the great expanse of ocean. Gus enjoys the spitting sea-air, sucking it into his lungs. He entwines his fingers with Miss Kilroy as they look over the tossing waves. He imagines the depths of the sea, the vulnerability of the ferry. It excites him.

Gus notices the cars whizzing around on the boreens as soon as he alights, their windscreens pleasantly bare from such irritations as NCT tests, insurance and tax. He likes it. He guesses you could probably use green diesel here too, without any concerns.

The Kilroy home is a small cottage to the west of the island, whitewashed with a slate roof which was once thatched, she tells him. Miss Kilroy's mother speaks with a strong island accent, a lilting tone which pierces the air. Her voice is deeper than Miss Kilroy's, it seems to have gathered weight with age. She feeds them beef stew and potatoes. She is a better cook than his mother. In Miss Kilroy's old bedroom, a small pile of paintings are stacked on a windowsill.

'Who did these?' Gus asks. He looks closely at the paintings.

'When I was a kid,' Miss Kilroy says.

They go to the local pub that night and listen to some local musicians. Her bed is lumpy but he is happily distracted from any material concerns. In the morning the island air tastes sweet.

Monday is spent nailing the new galvanise sheets to the rafters. The clouds are gathering, the rain is not far off. Tired he goes to bed early. A huge shoot-out on *The Dukes of Hazzard* wakens him at half three. He scribbles words in his notebook, the makings of a poem: 'Night, Sleep, Father, Gun.'

At about half ten next morning, he can go no further without washers. He does not feel like driving into town to get some. He walks up the boreen to Stephen's house. The house is built near the road and overlooks everyone who passes. Neighbours joke that Stephen can tell what shoppers have in the bags such is his vantage point. He is out in the perfectly manicured lawn, wrestling with a garden hose. He looks up as Gus approaches.

'Well.'

'Well.'

'Have you any washers?'

'Maybe.'

Stephen goes around the back of the house. Gus hangs back, looking around the perfect garden. One of the girl's trikes is parked awkwardly at the corner of the house.

Stephen returns with a little plastic bag of washers.

'How many is there?'

'I don't know,' he replies, with some irritation.

'Is this what ye are at?'

They turn to see their father across the road. 'What are you doing out?'

'I just said I'd have a walk.' He is smiling for once.

It is weeks, if not months since their father was out for a walk, something he had been doing for years up until recently. And he rarely smiled either. He turns away, hobbling back up the boreen to the cottage.

'What's the matter with him?' Gus says, eventually.

'I don't know. They're all I have anyway.'

'That's all?'

'That's all. Look, I've to get on with this.'

'Oh right. I can see you're fierce busy.'

'What do you mean?'

'What are you doing, sprinkling the daffodils?'

'There hasn't been a drop of rain for weeks if it's anything to ya.'

'You could gimme a hand with this shed.'

'Why would I do that?'

'Seeing as it belongs to ya?'

'Oh it does, does it? If that's the case, aren't you living in my house rent-free, so?'

Gus' eyes get foggy. He throws the washers to the ground and walks off stamping every step. Out of the corner of his eye he can see Stephen shaking his head as he attaches the hose to his precious garden tap. Gus picks up a stick off the boreen as he walks, calmer now, and begins to swing it as he had done as a child. Rent-free. That had stung.

In the evening Gus meets Miss Needham in The Postman. Her blonde hair is tied back. Her eyes are rounder than they were, he thinks. She is tired. Reilly is playing pool with an imaginary opponent. A film trailer catches his attention on the TV in the bar. It is about a policeman who bends the law to get his way. A trip to the cinema is arranged on Friday.

After midnight, as he slides naked into Miss Needham's single bed, the wind blows a small breeze through the galvanise sheets, left in suspended animation against the old mass concrete walls. The clouds begin to meet each other, and then the first drops of water fall from the sky, through the half-bolted rafters and onto old man Watt's sods of turf.

Back at the cottage next morning, there is uproar.

'What kind of man would go at that and rain promised, hah?'

'Sure you should have got Twomey, he'd have it done by now,' his mother adds.

'No, he had to go at it, and look at them sods bleddy soaked now, I don't know!'

Gus smiles at his parents as he eats his cornflakes. His headphones were probably the best present he had ever gotten. He had known he would need them as soon as he woke up that morning and looked out the window at the relentless rain. Chet Baker's 'It Never Entered My Mind' provides an ideal buffer to the onslaught.

'It's just the top skin that got it,' he says, guessing a break has arrived in the bombardment by the pursing of lips and intermittent shaking of heads.

'Top skin me arse!' his father says, banging his walking stick off a bucket, in a lightly-touched ambiguous way, somewhere between accident and fury.

Gus moves the top rows of soaked sods to one side and pulls an old silage cover over the rest. The rain is persistent. He is thoroughly soaked after twenty minutes.

'You might as well bring me for the pension, now,' his mother shouts from the kitchen.

The street is busy. Pensioners queue in the post office. Delivery men are double-parked outside the shops. Dunleavy leans on the windowsill of The Postman, smoking a cigarette.

Gus finds a parking space near the post office and waits as his mother slowly gets out of the car carrying her little green pension book. He observes some teenagers wandering up from the school to the shop for an eleven o'clock sausage roll. A pensioner passes by, hitting the pavement with his walking stick.

Frank Deane's silver Mercedes smoothly pulls up nearby. He gets out and despite Gus staring blankly at the foot well, walks over waving. Gus notices moccasins and brown cords. His hair even seems to have an American sheen, out of place in the Atlantic-beaten earth he stands on.

'Hey, how are you doing, Gus?' he says in his thick Nevada desert accent. Gus winds the window down slowly.

'Not too bad Frank, not too bad.'

'Coming to me party on Saturday night?'

'Oh yeah, what's that?'

'Bit of a shindig. Few musicians. Look, real sorry, I can't stay and chat, I've my realtor to meet. See you Saturday night!' We call them estate agents here, Gus thinks.

His mother returns, slowly waddling up the street to the car. She complains of an awful queue and not half enough staff there. They drive down the street to the supermarket. He parks near the entrance. Dunleavy has returned to his place within The Postman. Gus observes the lake flowing beneath the bridge. A fishing village it had been, that was its main attraction. But it had never really become a town. Still was not much more than a village really. It was not sure of itself, was it a town or a village? His mother comes out with two loaded bags and Gus gets out and helps her put them in the boot.

'Your boot is a lot smaller than Stephen's,' she complains.

'I don't need a big boot, do I?' he retorts. 'He has a big scatter of children.'

They drive back, his mother recounting the various people she encountered in the aisles. Mrs. Miggins had got very old looking, apparently. Poor old Tommy Cooke with the hump in his back, ah he's a lovely fellow, Tommy you know. Very kind. He got me the good tomatoes from the higher shelf. Very nice man.

'Will you slow down a bit, Augustus?'

'I'm doing twenty-five miles an hour.'

'You can't be too careful.'

'No.'

They unload everything into the kitchen. Gus' father watches the goods coming from the bags. 'Who eats mushroom soup here?' he mutters.

'You never said anything again it before.'

'I never ate mushroom soup. And them aul' sausages. Why didn't you get the good quality ones?'

'They are good quality. Do you see the price on them?'

The rain has stopped. It is too late in the day now to get anything done on the roof, he decides, and he walks down the boreen, leaving the bickering couple arguing about the freshness of Joyce's turnips.

He comes to Stephen's house. The two girls are playing catch in the garden.

'Have ye no school today?' he asks.

'Half day,' they say. 'Meeting.'

'Oh. Do ye want to come for a walk?'

There is a little boreen down the side of Stephen's house that loops the bog which is ideal for such uses.

'Okay.'

'Okay, well go in and tell your Mam.'

They run into the house and come back seconds later, running ahead down the boreen. The girls want to pick every colourful thing they see in the bushes that run alongside.

'Can we eat the blackberries?' they ask.

'You can,' he says. 'Just red berries, don't eat them, they're poisonous.'

The girls quickly fill their hands with fistfuls of blackberries and want Gus to do the same. He takes as many as he can hold.

'You should have brought a bucket,' he says.

'Why didn't you tell us?' they say. Marvellous how children can turn the tables. Just like women, really, he thinks. His phone rings. He piles the blackberries on top of a flat stone on the wall. It is Miss Kilroy.

'How are you, Mary?'

'Grand, were you coming to town tonight?'

'Yeah, I was going to.'

'It's just that I've got a meeting late, a work thing.' Oh. Making last minute changes. Not liking this.

'Oh. Well.'

'Maybe we could do something Friday, you know I've aerobics tomorrow.' Friday. Miss Needham and the cinema.

'There's this eejit home from America, he's throwing a party Saturday night, maybe we could go to it? Probably Stephen won't be around Friday for the bingo run.'

'Yeah, sounds good. So what are you doing?'

'I have the nieces out walking, they're picking flowers...'

'Oh, that's lovely.' But the 'lovely' was a little too maternal.

The children are pulling up leaves and flowers. One of the girls, the older one, makes the flowers into a little bouquet and hands it to Gus when he eventually puts his phone away.

'For your girlfriend,' she says.

'What girlfriend?' Gus asks.

'Daddy says you have a girlfriend.'

'Does he now?'

'He told Mammy last night, you look happy, you must have a girlfriend.'

'Ah.'

They get to the half-way mark on the loop and they complain their legs are tired. He tells them it will not be long now. They are dropping some of the blackberries.

'What can we do with the blackberries, Gus, can we eat them?'

'You can, yeah. And you can make jam from them.'

'Can you? Make jam? Oh!' They are very excited about this. They run towards home when they see it. Gus thinks about stopping to talk to Stephanie. He can see her washing up at the sink, her hair neatly pinned around her head. He decides against it. The girls safely back in the garden, he waves at them, and still carrying the bouquet for his girlfriend, returns back down the boreen. He slows near the old hayfield. He leans at the rusty gate and stands there, thinking of years gone by. As a child helping his father and grandfather loading bales. Later becoming strong and building the load himself. His grandfather dead some years now, was quite old at that stage. 'You done well today,' he remembers him saying. His father moaning about Stephen being away in boarding school. Gus had not gone to boarding school. Something about grades in sixth class and he had gone to the Tec. over in the coastal town.

So he looks happy, does he? Shows all that fella knows.

6

Gus spends Thursday wrestling with the new rafter. It is quite warped, he eventually realises, but he cannot face bringing it all the way back to exchange it for another. He has considerable trouble lining it up in accordance with the other rafters. Exasperated at four o'clock, he abandons it. However, his parents seem pleased.

'Looking better,' his mother comments.

'Couldn't be much worse,' his father adds, with an extremely vague hint of fondness.

In the evening his mood is dark. He listens to Dave Brubeck's 'Angel Eyes' on his phone. He is absorbed in the tune, in the way it dances around his consciousness, delving within, loosening all his worries and strains, relaxing him, helping him to fade into a dreamless sleep.

By Friday evening, he has half of the new sheets on. The movie is a disappointment. The policeman is more of a gangster than a law enforcer. He is despicably likeable. Gus is furious at this representation. Miss Needham finds this quite amusing. In the morning, they drive to the coastal town.

It is populated with pensioners, chewing gum chewing teenagers, gossiping make-upped wives and screaming children. Miss Needham wears a one-piece polka dot skirt over white heels. Her brown eyes seem to look straight through his grin. O'Leary, a square-faced farmer who Gus had done some fencing for, saunters along. His hat is awkwardly cocked on his flat head. He bobs up and down as he approaches.

'Gus,' he announces as the couple come into view.

'Out for the day?' Gus says.

O'Leary smells of beer and cabbage. His jaw is a mixture of rough and smooth where he had tried to shave that morning, giving it the effect of an atlas.

'Had to get a tap in Maloney's' he says, seeming to leap from one paving slab to the other.

'Huh?'

'For the fecking sink, gone arseways.'

'Oh.'

'And who is this fine woman?' O'Leary looks closely at Miss Needham, examining her like a pathologist might inspect a corpse.

'Hmm,' he eventually mutters, as though finding an element of the subject he couldn't quite explain.

'Nice to meet you,' Miss Needham says during the examination.

'Have you any children?' O'Leary says eventually, eyeing her hips.

They leave O'Leary without further ceremony. Miss Needham sees a shop full of antiques and they enter. The shelves are packed with clocks, fans, mirrors, shiny plastic moulds that do not have an obvious function. Gus enjoys watching Miss Needham slowly walk along the shelves looking at each item. He tries to guess what will catch her eye, something glittery, perhaps, something old, something moulded, something carved. He imagines her thoughts as she picks up an item, looks at it, sometimes even sniffs it, feels it and places it back delicately where it was.

'Nice isn't it?' she says, turning her head slightly to him. Her heels give her an extra three inches of height. He looks at the tiny square of floor the base of them claim.

'Yeah, very nice,' he says, with no idea what item she is referring to. At that moment he is truly in love with Miss Needham.

They eat at The Port, overlooking the flowing water of the river the town is built on. He eats lasagne and chips, she, salmon and rice. They watch the relentless traffic crawling by the pub window. Gus drives out through a windy road and they park on the pier, near the sea water. Seagulls fly in the distance over a bobbing sailboat in the horizon. He holds her hand as they walk along.

'It's lovely out here,' she says, and they kiss, a long deep kiss.

He tries to concentrate on the road as they drive back to her house where he knows they will go to bed to make long passionate love, and the enormity of the evening stretches out before him, having to get up shortly after, give her what she feels and describes as that deserted feeling, and go and play the second half. His phone is off, so there will be no distracting messages, he cannot even think about that other woman, her face, or anything about her, while he is with Miss Needham, for the neutral, she is winning this round but there is a long night ahead.

When he gets back to the cottage in the evening, his father is trying to fill a pipe with a piece of tobacco at the kitchen window. He coughs deeply.

'Sit down,' he says, as Gus arrives. Gus looks at him, somewhat taken aback. It is not in his father's nature to give orders directly, he usually prefers to criticise other's movements after they had completed them, while immediately noting on a more productive course of action that should have been taken.

'I know what you're at,' he says sharply, as Gus looks around for a cup.

'Is all that bag gone?' Gus says, looking in the nitrogen sack which has just a large pile of turf mould at the bottom. He takes up the poker and, lifting the lid off the range, pokes around at the embers. 'I'll get another bag.'

'Sit down.'

Gus feels as though he is ten and being accused of smoking a cigarette in the hayshed.

'I want to talk...ughhuh, huh, huh, ughhuh, ughhuhuhuh!'

'Jesus, are you aright there?'

'No, I'm not, can't ya see that! Now sit down!'

'What's wrong with you?'

'Listen. I know what you're at and it's all goin' to come to a head.'

'What are you on about?'

'You're up to no good!'

'What?'

'Don't annoy me!'

Gus' mother enters just then with a pile of dishcloths.

'Will you bring in another bag of turf, Gus?'

'I was just going to, I–'

'Sit down!'

His mother leaves, not waiting for any response, even if one was likely to arrive.

'Look, I told you now.'

He has the pipe filled and, tapping against the table, he lights it with an Ibiza cigarette lighter he found somewhere. The pleasant smelling pipe smoke fills the air.

'Mind yourself, lad. Ughhuhhuhu. Mind yourself. Be careful. Ughhuhuh. Ughuhuh. Be careful...'

His father launches into a vigorous coughing session which lasts two minutes.

'Do you want a drop of water?'

The question is ignored. His father eventually stops coughing and resumes sucking on his pipe. Gus always feels he looks something like a baby sucking a bottle in this position.

There is ten minutes of silence and Gus leaves the kitchen for the turf. When he returns, his father has left the kitchen.

'He's gone to bed,' his mother says as she enters. 'Not himself at all.'

Gus lies on his bed and examines his watch. He brings it out to the small bathroom and begins polishing it with an old toothbrush. Eventually all of the little black dots of dirt are gone. A feeling emerges from the pit of his stomach. How does his father know about the two Marys? Pub talk? His father has not been in the pub for weeks. Not able for any more than an odd half-one. Who has called to the house? He does not know who comes when he is out.

Gus drives slowly over the village to the church on the hill. Light flickers out from the houses. His mother is already saying the rosary as she feeds each bead through her hands. He sees the two old brothers cycling to mass, their spotlights already turned on, the year is moving toward winter. In the church, some pensioners are there since half seven, muttering prayers incomprehensible to everyone but them and their God.

After the mass. Gus sends a text to Miss Needham: 'Mother wants to go to Liam's for a sherry. Half hour. I will call around as soon as I can get away. Gxx.' He knew he would be 'delayed' and call her in the morning. This was not ideal but it would surely iron itself out soon.

Gus and Miss Kilroy drive up to Frank Deane's mansion overlooking the town. There is a crowd already inside. They walk up the marble steps. Gus rings the large door bell. Deane comes after a few moments.

'Hey guys! How are you Gus?'

A big shake-hands. He even goes so far as to kiss Miss Kilroy on the cheek.

'Any opportunity,' he jokes, giving Gus a playful punch in the ribs.

'Careful now,' Gus says, feeling like smacking Deane in the jaw. They enter the large hall.

'Can I take your jackets?' Deane says and helps Miss Kilroy with her light wrap.

It is then Gus feels very unwell. As he stands in the hallway, his vision extends through to Deane's large dining room. Standing at an enormous table loaded with savoury bites, his eyes widening at the expanse of the spread, is O'Leary. Gus involuntarily coughs loudly. He looks left, keep looking left.

'That's a fine room,' Gus says looking into Deane's unlit drawing room.

'Yeah, the drawing room, I might open it later if there is a huge crowd. Come on Mary, meet all the village folks.'

'We will now in a minute,' Gus says hanging back not really knowing what else to do.

'Come on, what's wrong with you?' Deane continues playfully.

'What's wrong?' Miss Kilroy says softly.

O'Leary has moved to the other end of the table. Gus slowly walks forward. The dining room is decorated with ornate cornices, thick Belgian carpet, white panelling below cream wallpaper. O'Leary deposits crackers, smoked salmon, cream cheese and glasses and glasses of wine down his throat at the other end of the table at a remarkable pace. Gus can feel his heart beating. Miss Kilroy has her hands in his. Other villagers are here. He really should have thought this through. Other villagers may have been in the coast town today, may have seen him with Miss Needham. This was not good.

'We'll sit down,' he says, and leads her to a vacant two-seater sofa beneath a stuffed moose's head.

'Is this the mystery lady?' Mrs. Hook says, as they reach the corner. 'Well, Gus, aren't you going to introduce me?'

'Oh yes, hello, Mrs. Hook. This is Mary Kilroy.'

'Hello Mary, how are you?'

'I'm fine, and yourself?'

'Great now. Are you on holidays?' Because of course I pick up all the tourist tail in this place, Gus moans to himself.

'No, I'm on work here. I'm in the civil service.'

'Oh. Civil service? Oh. I see,' Mrs. Hook cannot help her eyes switching to Gus for a split second. What's wrong with you, Gus would like to say. 'Well, that's a good permanent job.'

'Mmm.'

At the door Gus sees Deane welcoming Miss Needham and another lady, equally as attractive.

'I'll get another drink,' Gus says and hurries away through the crowd toward Deane's big ground floor toilet. The bathroom is enormous, the size of his sitting room in the cottage. It has a large free-standing bath and a huge sink with gold-painted taps. Everything gleams white. He stares in the mirror. He had missed one nose hair. He wets his finger and pushes it back up his nostril. Perhaps he will be able to sneak back to his seat without being noticed. Miss Needham will surely go to the table for a few moments.

Perhaps he could say to Miss Kilroy he has a headache and they might leave. It seems a bit puffy but he should never have come in the first place. He takes a deep breath. He slowly opens the door to find Miss Needham standing outside.

'How are ya?' he smiles broadly. He reaches to kiss her but she retracts.

'What happened to your mother?'

'She didn't want to go to the pub, I met Deane and sure I had to call down for a quick one. I was going to call over to you after. Load o' shite, sure.'

'Oh right. I'll be out in a second.' She enters the bathroom, shutting the door, and Gus is left in the hall alone. While he stands there, it is like his life has gone into suspended

74

animation, he can think of nothing, no scheme to escape from the imminent catastrophe, no possible solution, he cannot move. Really, what he should do is run out the back door, run and run until he gets home and, safely back with his parents in the cottage, get into his bed, go asleep. She returns, a fresh scent of perfume around her.

'I think I see someone I know in the kitchen,' Gus says, sweating. They enter the granite-clad kitchen. A colourful group talk, laugh and drink. No sign of Miss Kilroy at least. She is still on the two-seater sofa. Gus can sense that Miss Needham is speaking to him but he is distracted. They are now in the company of Mrs. Hook. Gus tries to stand slightly away from Miss Needham. This is not easy but he might pull it off.

'That's a lovely girl you have there, Gus,' Mrs. Hook is saying. Miss Needham nods, smiles, and drinks her drink. 'I don't think I've had the pleasure.'

'How are you? Mary Needham.'.

'Are you a friend of Frank's?'

'Well, I came up with Jenny from the clinic…'

'Mmm, well, tell Mary I was delighted to meet her,' Mrs Hook says to Gus and wanders off.

'What was that about?' Miss Needham says.

'Alzheimer's,' Gus replies promptly.

He feels like he is on a sinking ship and he is searching for the last life boat. The people around him are relaxed, enjoying the camaraderie. Deane arrives in the kitchen. Gus is unsure, so confused now, he does not know which Mary he introduced as his girlfriend. Miss Needham goes to the kitchen table and pours a glass of wine.

Deane looks around, nodding at guests, giving the occasional thumbs-up signal. Gus' neck becomes itchy. 'Ah, I'll miss the place when I go back to the states,' Deane says.

'When are you going back?'

'Monday week friend, I'm afraid. That's a fine woman you got there.'

'Not too bad now.'

'And another fine one out in the dining room.' He guffaws, bending over with mirth. 'Heh, heh. Fair play to you. No better man to pull it off. But it could get a bit messy. I wouldn't have brought both of them here but...'

'I didn't–'

'There you are!' Miss Kilroy arrives between them. 'Where did you go to?'

Gus is afraid to look around. 'I'm not feeling the best,' he says. 'Will we get a bit of air?'

'Just dive out through them patio doors,' Frank Deane says helpfully.

In the cool air outside, the moon lights up the temporary smoker's gazebo. Music blasts from the house.

'Oh, I love that song, come on, let's have a dance...' Miss Kilroy says, taking Gus's hand.

'I don't really feel like it.' She drags him in and he is on the floor.

He dances with her, twirling her around. While her back is turned, he keeps an eye on Miss Needham's dress, a small triangle of which he can see in the kitchen. The dance floor is an impromptu set-up in the middle of the dining room, the grand table slightly pushed toward a corner.

'I need a drink,' Miss Kilroy says, laughing, and walks through the heaving crowd toward the kitchen.

'Gus!' Miss Needham says from behind him and grabs Gus' hands. He dances another song with Miss Needham. He whispers to her he has a sore hip and needs to sit down.

He will have to get out of here soon, his heart is thumping, and he is starting to have double vision. He uses the toilet excuse and escapes the dining room.

Gus meets Peadar out in the hall. Peadar is a tall man wearing an old jacket which has been worn to club meetings in the 1970s, discos in the 1980s, funerals and weddings in the 1990s and now makes regular appearances at late-night pub drinking and card games. He considers Gus' sweating demeanour. 'Ah Gus…well, how are things? Up to your old tricks, are you?'

'Not really,' Gus replies, wiping his nose. He looks around, there is a brief respite in the music.

'Are you under a bit of pressure there, Gus?'

'Ah, just a bit off, I think.'

'Something you ate maybe? The quails' eggs, what are they? Deane was on about them. Did he bring them back from Texas?'

'Las Vegas.'

'Uh?'

'Las Vegas he's in.'

'Las Vegas? Beyont in America? Well. Do they have them quare things there, do they?'

'I don't know, Peadar. They must have.'

'How is the caravan going?'

'Uh– not too bad.'

'Are you going living in it?'

'No. Just using it for, you know. Storage.'

'And why have you it in the forest?'

'Ah, it's just handier there.'

'But what about the shed? And why have you the roof took off the shed, in this type of weather your turf will be soaked, hah?'

Gus goes back outside to the night and the gazebo. He sits on a garden chair. Through the window Gus sees Deane has his huge arms around two of his guests, Miss Kilroy and Miss Needham.

He is purple-faced with mirth. He squeezes the two women, twisting his waist this way and that. Gus tries to read Deane's lips as he speaks. It could not be anything too detrimental, as both women are smiling and nodding.

'Are you alright, there?'

Gus turns around. McCluskey. He holds a pint glass of cider and his other hand swings as though unsure what to do without a trowel. 'Is it yourself? I didn't see you.'

'What are you at?'

'Fresh air.'

'Ah.'

'Fine set up.'

'Oh yeah, Deane knows how to throw a do.'

'He does. Did you try the grub?' Gus blurts out.

'Arragh, a bit of it aright. Posh ol' shit.'

Peggy Hegarty, a stretched-looking woman of late forties, walks around the corner of the house. She breaks into a smile.

'Gus, how are you!' Her hand shakes Gus' like a wiry claw, grabbing and sucking the blood from him. She nods at McCluskey and slips inside.

'You didn't get the shake hands,' Gus says.

'That ol' bitch, she wouldn't pay up for a job a few years ago. Reckoned one of the walls was cracking. Well, I have to see O'Leary about a shed that needs plastering.' McCluskey disappears into the house. Gus sits in the moonlight which has emerged from the late evening clouds.

7

Stephen comes out. He is slightly shook looking, possibly worse for wear after numerous cans of Deane's lager. 'Are you aright?'

'Fine.'

'What are you up to, Augey?'

'Nothing.'

Gus felt himself adopting the sheepish expression of one who has stolen from the biscuit box.

'There is women involved.'

'There is no women involved.'

'That's a fine lady I saw you with earlier.' Gus wonders which fine lady he means.

'You were dancing together. Fine bit of stuff. I–' Stephen's phone rings. He answers it, turning toward the road. Seconds later, he hangs up. 'We have to go.'

'Why?'

'We have to go, come on.' Stephen is already striding across the hall through the revellers. Gus hurries to catch up with him as they reach the front door.

'What is it?' But he already knows.

'It's the old lad. He collapsed in the house. He could be…I don't know.'

Gus follows Stephen out, the whole night pouring down the sinkhole of importance. Miss Kilroy, Miss Needham, the hiding out in different rooms, guarded conversations, toilet breaks, mirrored discussions with himself, they all fade into meaninglessness around this sudden news. The coughing, the spluttering, the slower walking, the lying later in bed, it all began to make sense.

A few of the party-goers turn and look as the brothers walk out. In the side of his eye, Gus can see whispering, talking, word was travelling fast, it depended on who had rang Stephen, it might be Stephanie. She would be discreet but if it was one of the neighbours, everyone would know.

'Come on!' Stephen shouts at Gus loudly, the harshness of his voice shattering the party atmosphere, he bared his teeth as he had shouted, the animalism of it shook Gus into action. As Gus gets into the car, he hears O Leary asking what is going on, his mouth still full of vol-au-vents.

The hospital is very quiet at four in the morning. They had to go through the Casualty section to get into the main hospital and their father. Across from the reception desk a man speaks quietly to himself and a woman reads a magazine beside a sleeping child. Sluggish porters push large trolleys of items, sheets, pillows, bottles, along the wide silent corridors. With the outside light gone everything glows artificially. The smell invades his lungs, which an hour earlier had inhaled the fumes of cigar smoke and rich wine.

They eventually reach the waiting area outside the Intensive Care unit. Only one allowed in at a time, Stephanie says. Gus sees his mother through the glass, sitting on the bed. Her eyes are wet, she holds her rosary beads, she mutters a constant prayer. He can only see the outline of his father's still body. There is one other patient within, some relatives sit across from the Watts.

'I left the kids at McGovern's,' she tells Stephen.

It is four forty five.

Stephanie tells them her mother called her at two saying Jimmy had fallen out of the bed. He was unconscious. Now he lay in the bed and was under observation. Information was cryptic from the doctors. They said it was probably a stroke, but they would need to do tests.

Gus stares out at the lights of the county town. Even at this hour there is some movement. Taxis, mini-buses, the silhouettes of late-night revellers.

Eight missed calls. He checks his messages. 'U ok? Mxx.' 'What is it? M'. It would seem they had not yet had a close tete-to-tete. Just as well that was not something he had to face tonight. But it is getting closer too. Everything is imminent. His father's death. His discovery. His singledom again. Change is always on the horizon. There is no avoiding it, no matter what one does.

He wants to get out of here. He is tired. He does not hold out any hope. His father's time is up, it seems.

He leans against the cold wall behind him. Stephen stares ahead. Stephanie reads a magazine she has picked up from the table next to her.

He begins to doze. The strange unpredictable noises of the hospital keep sporadically reawakening him. The air conditioning hums above. There is a movement of a trolley somewhere. The occasional shout from the Casualty waiting room. He hears breathing. Gus imagines it is his father's breathing slowing down.

He considers the family across the way, not much different to his own. A harassed-looking woman in her late fifties. A similar-aged man dozes. A child of about five plays with a doll. Within the unit, Gus can see a woman in her early thirties, sitting beside the patient.

Gus feels this would be a good scene for a poem, the three of them in the waiting area, looking across at three other people. He could call it 'The Final Departure'.

He knows his father would like to be in the little cottage forever, criticising what Gus does, and his mother, moaning about the weather, the football team. The government.

Frank Deane arrives. He is suitably transformed from the exuberant handshaking host to subdued sympathetic figure. He is even wearing a darker coat and whispers instead of shouts. It is almost as though he is already at the funeral.

'An awful do,' he croaks as he meets Gus.

'Thanks for coming, Frank.'

'Oh, not at all, not at all. I remember when my old man passed on a few years ago, I was glad of the support.'

Gus wants to say his father is not dead, not yet, but Deane has speeded everything up since he went to the states. Everything seems to move faster out there, but here in the old country, things develop at a different pace. The only thing they do here quicker than anyone else is bury their dead. But it is morbid to be thinking of such things. Deane tries to retract what he said, noting Jimmy's strong heart and great will power. Good few years left there yet, he says eventually. Gus wonders why Deane is here, nobody else had come, they have enough cop on to realise this is a family time, this could be the end of his father and people are leaving the family to themselves. But not Deane. For some reason, he felt he had to attend and be a sort of proxy village watcher.

They stand outside, in a small courtyard area. Deane lights a small cigar.

'Bad do about that lad an' all,' he says, nodding towards the unit, breathing out the thick fumes.

'What happened him; he's only a young fella is he?'

'Stabbed on the main street a couple of hours, I don't know what the place is coming to. You see it out in the states, but not around here, you don't expect that.'

'Jays and where were the boys in blue, never there when you need them, hah?' Gus says.

'That's just it–'

The man in his fifties emerges at the door, nodding at Gus and Deane, taking out a cigarette. Deane tosses the half-smoked cigar to the ground.

'Look, I better leave ye to it. If there's anything I can do...'

Gus takes his seat again and lies his head back on the cold windowsill behind. His mind fades in and out of sleep. All at once he is dreaming about a bizarre battle where he is amongst a Napoleonic war; his father is a General leading the warriors into battle. There are flashes of light and he wakes up again. It is getting bright outside. The door opens and his mother emerges from the unit. It is his turn to go in.

The unit is a peculiar experience. The other empty beds seem ghastly, as though their patients have already progressed to the mortuary, and their blankets are now awaiting the next late-night victim. His father is in the far corner, the further end of the room. He passes the other patient. Gus sees a blue uniform messily piled on the locker, a Garda badge gleams on the front of a hat at the bottom of the bed. His wife holds the man's hand and stares into his face, his upper lip trembles slightly.

Gus gets to his father's bed and takes the seat, still warm from his mother. He looks at his father, eyes closed, mouth also open and a tube attached to his left nostril. Computer screens beep beside him. An intravenous tube is connected through a needle in his wrist.

His father looks strange with all this technology inserted in him, out of place, as though the blanket should be patterned and the tubes should be coloured silage-cover black, instead of clinical white.

There is no sound except the continual beeping of the machine and the faint intake of breath. He sits there for fifteen minutes. He gets up and walks out past the Guard and his wife who has not moved. He comes out and looks at Stephanie who reluctantly puts down the magazine and goes in. His mother is sitting, holding her bag, staring at the wall. He thinks she looks like she is waiting for a bus.

'Do you want to come home?' he says. She shakes her head. He leaves the hospital.

The clouds are beginning to separate, the first cracks of the sun emerge. The man he saw earlier is leaving the casualty room, still muttering to himself, with his arm bandaged. The woman and child are gone. Gus gets into his car and drives home listening to 'When Sunny Gets Blue'.

The house is strange without them in it. Everything within is somehow more noticeably still, like it has been abandoned in a hurry, which of course it has. He sits for a while on the chair and another poem arrives in his mind. 'The morning rises, the parents leave, the son sits helpless on the chair.'

He yawns. He will do the herding for Stephen; the old annoyance seemed to have drifted temporarily away. He does not mind about the land going to his brother. Maybe this has been the problem all along, that he has felt trapped with his parents. Maybe he needed them out of the house to realise that.

Outside the air is cool, the autumn has definitely arrived. His jacket is a bit light. He walks alongside Stephen's fields. The land is all joined together, most of it can be accessed by a convoluted network of boreens. It runs back from the cottage for thirty acres, the land disintegrates in quality until the last pieces are just fit for turf. Across the road beyond Stephen's house are a further ten. Gus climbs the fence and walks across the grass, his mind wandering carelessly, observing the contented munching of the cattle, the careful grass-picking of the sheep. He tries to count the ewes. They run around as he walks through them. He gets fifty-six the first time, fifty-eight the second, fifty-three the third.

He had brought Stephen's collie, Belle, who follows him around. He had given her a tin of Paws in an old bowl at the side of the house before they left. He hates the smell of dog food, hates forking it out onto the bowl. For a farmer's son, he is strangely squeamish. Even though they always said to him he had ideal small thin fingers. Pulling lambs, he had done occasionally, he would not like to see a lamb or sheep die on his watch. But he had to close his eyes and somehow try to forget what he was doing. And force his fist into the back of the ewe, feel around in the tight vacuum, trying not to think of early dating experiences until he somehow grapples a pair of hooves and a head and, bringing them together, tries to draw them out. A 'couple' made things even more complicated. One might die, the one that was left while the other was being pulled.

If his father or Stephen were faced with a lamb the wrong way, they would reach their arm in, turn it around, it sometimes happened. But Gus would call the vet if he was in that predicament. It was never said, never mentioned that he always called the vet, but he knew it. Sometimes a lamb was dead in the womb, had been dead for a day. The smells alone were enough to make him puke. It was risky to wait for the vet in this case. The gas of dying flesh exuded out into the air, and the animal made grotesque noises as Gus would have to try and draw the dead lamb out. It had to be done or the sheep would die also as she could not yean herself. It was work he despised. But it was work he was given to do.

He had to do it, because it was his duty. Until the farm had been given to Stephen. Then he was free of it. But yet he had somehow been mad about it.

'I'm giving the land to Stephen,' his father had said one day after Mass. That was it. No more than that. Gus could not even muster up the words, I might have known. Or even Why?

Why are you giving it all to Stephen? Is that fair, do you think? What about me?

He was able to sign on the dole at eighteen without the complications of land attached to his name.

He had visions of being a poet. He had moved to the coastal town and got a flat with some other apprentice life-wanderers. After a year of pool-playing, gambling and occasional labouring work to supplement his payment, he had met Sandra.

He sits in the kitchen, while Belle slurps milk from an old frying-pan outside. He boils himself an egg, listening to the long weather forecast. There is something relaxing about the tone of the forecaster. Inland areas. Rising slowly. North Head, Old Head, South Head. Pressure. Highest temperatures. Something comforting about hearing about all these remote places. Water brushing against cliffs at Old Head. Another poem. 'Crashing against the cliff, crashing and smashing.'

He had been too young really. There were two loves that time too, the lads and Sandra. He could not decide then either. Had he learned nothing? Another foolish use of luck. Sandra's father was in his late sixties. Gus had been handed the reins of the pub on the peninsula, installed as manager at nineteen. A beautiful girlfriend and a thriving business, what more could a young man ask for? He had gotten into poker schools, high-ticket pool competitions, all night boozing. The accounts after one year looked as though the receiver might be called in. Sandra's father had shown him the door.

'No land, nothing to my name,' he had said at the desk to the woman sitting beyond the glass on his return. She had nodded as she had probably nodded to thousands of others and she had taken his details, but Gus felt as he described his activities for the past years, there was a sense of sympathy that he had lost.

As he sits there, out of the blue a suffocating sadness falls all around him. He can feel his stomach churning as though someone has hit him with a blunt object. It is like a hammer blow.

He looks at his phone, there are no new messages. The women have given up. They have stopped contacting him. Have they spoken, he wonders? Have they gotten sick of his avoidance tactics? Is it his fault his father is dying? Surely they can be reasonable? No, it is early, they are probably asleep. He is too tired, his thinking is skewed. He sits staring out the window, feeling too lethargic to clear away the egg cup and plate. He dozes on the chair.

His mother arrives at eleven with Stephen. Stephanie is at the hospital. He observes his mother and feels it is like watching Laurel without Hardy. She does not seem to know where to sit in the house, what to say, who to lament. Now her husband is in the hospital, it is like he is already gone, out of their lives. She eventually sits across from the range in the visitor's chair.

He wants to say something to her, to comfort her maybe, but nothing will come out. All he can do is look out into the field, the clouds are gathering, it is a grey day.

Later, he goes back to the hospital. His father seems to have deteriorated more if that were possible. His face is now almost in the corpse position, chin lifted up higher than the forehead, mouth slightly open, eyes closed. Getting ready to leave, he thinks.

He rings Miss Needham at eight that evening. It is pot luck, he could have called either of them. She seems distant. Why, he wonders. He does not feel from her conversation that she knows anything. He will not ring Miss Kilroy straight after. He will leave it until the morning.

The days are different in this strange time he lives.

8

Gus dreams all kinds of crazy things, his father being dug up from the grave alive and returning to full health, Miss Needham and Miss Kilroy both coming up the aisle together, holding hands as they march in pristine white dresses. A Rolls-Royce waiting for the three of them, leaving the church with only two seats in the back and a big space in the middle, which Gus keeps sliding into, grappling each side to pull himself up. He wakes in a sweat.

The next day, his father is breathing more easily. A crisply-dressed doctor informs Stephen and Gus that he might even regain consciousness before the weekend. His father looks like a little boy spread out under the blankets. He hardly holds a form. It is as though he is sinking into the clinical mattress beneath.

After the doctor is gone, they sit in silence, listening to the beep of the machine.

'Theresa's lot are arriving at eleven, will you get them?' Stephen says eventually. Gus leaves, his feet squelching on the rubber floor.

There is some release in the fresh air. He absent-mindedly kicks a lone empty beer can along the path. Someone from Casualty the night before. He looks over at the entrance, imagining the scenes at the doorway. Looks so civilised during the day, yet at night, any number of incidents could break out. It is strange when the same place has a different atmosphere. He imagines how the cottage will change if the unthinkable happens. He wonders is he still holding on to some childish hope that everything will be alright, his father will be okay, everything will go on as normal. That nothing ends, everything goes on forever. It seems difficult to imagine the future, he who always thought ahead, the next stroke, the next girl, the next job.

It is an hour's drive to the airport. It is a small place, there is only one flight in the morning, from London. He sees his nephews first. Jonathan and Anderson are fighting over something, it looks like the aeroplane's vomit bag. Theresa wears a controlled frown. Over the years, she has developed an English accent which irks him. 'Heeelo'. 'Hew are you?'. 'Thenk you'. 'Foine'. 'Eeveerything is foine, meother'. 'Foine'. He muses how nobody ever returns with an adopted cockney accent. It is always the middle-class twang which seems to stick. 'Weonderful, ebsolutely weonderful'. 'Rathur!'. 'Rahtur!'

You were born at the butt-end of a mountain and don't forget it, Gus thinks. But he does not say anything. Ron bounds along, carrying a designer 'manbag', his disgustingly flat stomach and skating-rink hair a sublime aggravation. His jaw is perfectly smooth.

'How is the faurm?' Ron asks, as they drive out onto the main road. What farm? I don't have a farm, Gus fumes inwardly. He ignores the question. He drops them at the hospital.

'We ought to find a car to rent for a few days,' Ron says, as they get out.

'There was a Hertz office at the airport,' Gus announces curtly.

The showers clear in the afternoon and he decides he will tackle the rest of the roof sheeting. At least that would be a job done before his father gets out and sees it. He will tackle the job professionally, not half-heartedly, but without reserve. He will do this as though it is the most important job of his career.

On the roof he discovers another rafter looks too rotten to survive fifteen more winters. He should have checked them all out before going to Maloney's that day. He stares at the rotting timber with exasperation.

He takes out his phone. Through some technological conundrum the screen saver is a photo of the caravan, taken some weeks ago as part of the evidence for his application. He has not been out at the caravan since the meeting with Miss Kilroy. It may well have been overrun by forest wildlife at this stage. He should probably check it, he thinks, in case it is needed for any further interviews. However, it looks as though his application will be approved.

He rings Miss Needham. She seems distant. But still there are kisses at the end of the conversation. Miss Kilroy is the opposite. She seems if anything broody. She calls him 'love' repeatedly, a pet name she seems to have developed from somewhere. Avoiding the rotten rafter for today, he tacks on some more sheets, but is distracted. Ron and Theresa arrive in a rented car. Gus remains off ground level. They leave a short time later with his mother.

The cottage is empty and cold in the evening. He has a large bowl of cornflakes and lies on the bed. He listens to a version of 'Let's Get Lost' on his phone. He sleeps intermittently, dreaming again of his father. His mother will come home in the morning, he reads on a text message from Theresa.

Gus is in a deep sleep when his phone rings. His clock radio reads ten past four.

'You'd better come,' Stephen says. Everything is a blur as he hurries through the dark kitchen. The dawn is much later toward the end of September. He is cold as he comes outside the house. His anorak is loosely tossed around a white t-shirt. At the end of the road he meets Stephen, rolls down the window.

'What is it?' he asks, feeling fear in his voice, afraid to hear the answer.

'Don't know,' Stephen says. 'Theresa texted me to come, now. You can come with me.' Stephen's car is icily cold. Gus turns the heater on. Nothing happens until he turns the dial to four, when it makes a ferocious blowing noise. He turns it off immediately. There does not seem to be a place for noise in this morning.

Everything in the town is still, like statues. Cars parked at angles, bins stacked in corners, leaves unmoving on the trees in the town green. The rows of terraced houses cut a jagged outline in the cracking sky.

They arrive outside the hospital, the darkness is familiar now. A few figures again silhouette the entrance to Casualty. The lights burn into the night darkness. Through the cold corridors the men march, sweeping past doors, to the lift and up, up to Male Surgical.

He wants to sit down, to compose himself, to prepare for the inevitable, it seems certain now, but Stephen will not stop, continues to march on as though their father's life depended on their arriving on time.

They get to the dark ward, only a dull glow around his father's bed, and he knows immediately. His mother sits on a chair, her face ashen. Stephen stands looking at their father, a towel wrapped around his jaw to keep his mouth closed. Gus cries, holding the rail of the bed, as though hanging on, spluttering, shaking, whinging.

People shake Gus' hand, he is not sure who. He notices he is hugging his mother. He eventually sits on a chair near the bed. There is a long silence and the morning drifts to conversations he forgets instantly, repeated handshakes. The word 'arrangements' is whispered intermittently. The priest arrives. His sarcastic expression gone, he nods at Gus, lays out a purple cloth on the deceased, says some quiet words. He has left again in a few minutes.

At some stage, Gus does not know how much later, he walks outside to the car. The sun is at his back, the wind rustles through the soft green leaves in the trees. It is like a flame has been lit in his body and is beginning to burn through his internal organs, there will be nothing left of him only a hollow shell walking along the path with nothing to keep him from sliding down around the concrete, drifting down through the gravel beneath, seeping into the clay and disappearing forever into the deep dark ground.

9

The little blue van bobbles along the road. McCluskey sucks at his large mug of tea, while the radio blares through the open window. Gus looks outside intently as though there is an incredible scene playing before him in the rolling fields.

He had little idea how he had negotiated the funeral and the two Marys. It was a blur now of crowds, the church, the coffin, his father in the grave. There had been something amiss, however. He had ten missed calls (no messages) on his phone.

All became clear the following Friday. In the morning he had sat, alone in the kitchen. The smell of his father was still there. On the windowsill lay his pipe which he would never again smoke, on the door hung his jacket which he would never again wear.

Gus felt emptiness crawling up around his body, lifting the hairs on his skin. He could not avoid visualising his father sitting in the kitchen. His old head bobbing beside the range. His eyes on the yard at Gus hauling around galvanised sheets.

Gus had walked past the still unfinished shed roof. He could not return to it. The constant expectation of his father arriving at the door making comments meant Twomey would have to be called in to finish it. Another failed project.

The village street that morning was no busier or quieter than usual. O'Leary, spitting and spluttering outside Joyce's, as he sized up the weekly offers through the window. Mrs. Hook's voice wandered outside, criticising the butcher's latest prices on lamb chops. Franny Morrin had put in a difficult weekend with his leaf-blower, he informed Gus at length. 'There's no air in these new models, Augey! What are they doing with all the air?'

While on his way to place a bet in Keane's, he heard the unmistakeable yet horrifying sensation of Miss Needham and

Miss Kilroy's dulcet voices intermingling. He had made a decision to somehow break off with one of them at the weekend. They had spoken together before at Deane's party, and at various stages of the funeral, he was unclear as to what level. But there was a lower tone to their words which made him shiver. It was the emotional tone, the sensitive tone, the reveal-all-about-yourself tone. And they were speaking with each other.

He slowed down, afraid to walk anymore, as though he was trying to step forward against the current in the sea. He realised then he had reached The Country Kitchen window and they were sitting just inside the door.

The two Marys stared at him.

He stood there in a state of confusion, of immobility. It was like the horror film that he could not take his eyes off, yet was in absolute terror. The iridescence of the light somehow came through the window to illuminate his girlfriends as though they were apparitions, they were not real, this could not be real. He was having paranoid delusions; it was all a terrible, horrible uncouth nightmare that he wanted to wake from immediately.

Or was it? Miss Kilroy liked the Country Kitchen for coffee on her way to appointments in the region. So too, did Miss Needham in between patients. It was he who had introduced them to the place. O'Leary spluttered on in the background.

He closed his eyes.

Miss Needham got up suddenly, stormed to the door with a terrifyingly purposeful stride. He could see her whole demeanour had transformed, every nook and cranny had been devoured amongst the emerging embro-skeleton of scorndom, her eye sockets were like pebbles with little mouths, biting through the air at him. Then he saw the light of the street landed a perfect square white flag on her pupils, but there was no truce here, no meek surrender in this imminent encounter.

'Come in, we want to talk to you.' She went in and sat down again, opposite Miss Kilroy. Gus walked slowly to the door, feeling every step. Still in slow motion, in a state of jellied eeldom. He stood at the entrance. Miss Kilroy adopted no discernible expression. But he could see her lips were flat, liveliness quenched, her brown eyes glistened, they were moist.

He turned and walked quickly down the path, hearing the shouting, running, knocking over chairs. He broke into a run, not seeing where he was going, off balance, straight into the grey steel of the streetlight which had been receiving O'Leary's liquid shrapnel minutes earlier. He felt his ear being grabbed, a nail scratched his cheek, he wrestled, the whole street stopped, cars braking, windows rolling down, laughter, shouting, him shouting, them cackling, like all those morning birds in the mountain with a warped cello undertone beneath them. His jumper was pulled off in the struggle, it tore, their arms felt thin but wiry, really, really wiry. This could not be happening, it would never happen; women would not behave like this, like animals.

He remembers a girl pulling his hair when he was ten years old at a birthday party. It was a girl he liked, he had been watching her a lot in sixth class, it was more of a fascination than an attraction. She may have felt the same, pulling his hair; maybe it was her way of demonstrating it.

This was not affection though. He could feel it in their arms, the coldness of female provocation, absolute and complete viciousness. There was something, a bite, a need to cause pain in the way they grappled him at that moment. In seconds he was away from them, he was running, blood slipped around his eyelid and stung his eye. He saw Franny Morrin missing the whole fracas while lecturing the staring Mrs. Hook on the price of coal. He wished he was Franny, just at that moment.

The old couple in the car absorbed the whole scene. If they were novelists, they might have a litany of bestsellers. But they wrote nothing down, only chewed on it with their gums, teeth long gone.

He eventually got to his car; they were not far behind. What on earth did they think they would do to him? He was terrified, he felt like a child being bullied at school. The whole place was laughing at him, the sad drama played out in front of everyone in brutal clarity. He should never have looked at another woman; he should have got married in the Peninsula that time. If he had minded himself, none of this would have happened. He could have a fifteen-year-old son now. But the accountant, the rotten accountant had come and taken all that for himself, just another 'leg of his empire.' He remembers Peter's face as he said it, 'one of these hot-shots.' His vision was blurred as he drove away.

But that was a fantasy. That was what he wished had happened. That was what he invented the following nights, as he could not sleep, he felt he would never sleep again, felt like he was on fire, like he was burning at both ends.

The two Marys never looked up at the glass. After a few minutes they stood together, walked out the door of The Country Kitchen, passing Gus without a word, saying goodbye to each other, getting into their cars and driving off. Where was the hot female emotion? He could not provoke it. He instinctively took his phone out. There were no missed calls.

In the rumbling van, he feels acutely unwell. He wishes his dream was the reality and not the cold, almost careless dismissal of him. The only thing worse than being caught is being ignored.

There is little banter this morning. They drive south, through the centre of the county where the land quality improves, the rockiness fades from the fields, the grass begins to thicken and become lusher. In the south of the county, sheds are newer, cattle are healthier and more fed looking, fences are neater. The gorse of the north of the county fades, the landscape becomes dark green.

'Great land down here. Trying to make a farm pay in our place. We're not living at all behind in the sticks,' McCluskey says. Flags hang out of windows as they pass. The county team is preparing for the cup final.

'The land is great in the south and shite in the north,' Gus mutters as they arrive at the job; a sprawling bungalow miles from anywhere. His voice is somewhat slurred, he notices. 'They have the flag upside down. The green should be on the bottom.'

'Not really, there's no mistake in it.' McCluskey replies, taking his two large turkey sandwiches from the dusty dash. 'The green is always going to be above the red.'

Two hours later they are back in McCluskey's yard, examining a cow. McCluskey's father had called, thinking the animal was about to calve. She regurgitates contentedly, rubbing her quarters against the stone wall of the barn. She looks at Gus, her brown eyes questioning. Out of his normal habitat of bare block walls during the vital working hours, McCluskey becomes frantic at the loss of earnings.

'She's not ready. What's wrong, that fella must have Alzheimer's…all the way back for nawthin'. Diesel, a man out with me all day, nothing earned! Jesus! We'll…we'll do a few of the shelves she does be harping on about, come on!'

McCluskey collapses in his kitchen. It is like an avalanche, this colossal mound of flesh, unnaturally destabilising, crashing into the feeble kitchen table against the chairs, spreading down across the tiles, seeming to cover the whole floor. He froths at the mouth and rolls around onto his back.

Gus runs to the sink, deciding to fill a mug of water for some reason. He puts the cup down and calls an ambulance. He shakes McCluskey, his face is white. He cannot hear a heartbeat, he does not know how to check for a pulse.

The ambulance men come within fifteen minutes. McCluskey is not dead, they tell him. They lift his huge body onto a stretcher which bends under his weight. They ask Gus to get pyjamas, something for an overnight stay. Where is his wife? they ask. But McCluskey had insisted she went back to work after the sixth child started school.

Gus searches for pyjamas in the master bedroom; there is nothing in the wardrobe. He searches drawers, pulling out underwear, socks, t-shirts. One drawer at the bottom seems stuck; in his hurry, he tugs it aggressively. It gives way, cracking. A pile of letters slide out onto the floor. 'Hello darling,' the first line reads. Bemused, he picks it up. It is signed 'Peg'. It seemed the Owl man had been paid after all.

He puts the letters back and tries to refit the drawer. Eventually he finds a pyjama bottom under the bed beside a large plastic shopping bag full of green hundred euro notes. The ambulance drives off, leaving Gus alone in McCluskey's house.

The awareness of how much cash is likely to be hidden around the place makes him feel uneasy. He hurries across the boreen to the old house where McCluskey's parents live. McCluskey's mother is rolling dough on the kitchen table.

Gus leaves her shakily speaking on the phone and drives out the boreen, toward the county town. McCluskey's wife is already at the hospital when he arrives. She sits in the Casualty waiting room. She nods at Gus. Pleasantries have been abandoned in this world.

'They have to do tests,' she says, eventually.

Gus leaves after a few minutes. He returns to the cottage. He parks his car but does not get out. Through the back door, he can see Stephen is in the kitchen with his mother. He is applying the bunion cream to her feet. Gus sits watching. He looks up at the half-finished roof. After a while, Stephen and his mother come out the door and get into Stephen's large people–carrier. They drive out past Gus. Stephen waves at him casually.

Gus sits alone in the kitchen. Everything is collapsing, falling like the old plasterer, deteriorating before his eyes. He lies down on the floor. He feels like he is suffocating. Bright lights are flashing before him, strange shapes jump out of his eyes, he turns looking at the ceiling. In the house, his groans rattle around every wall.

'Lord almighty,' he shouts, as he crawls into the front room, the mat invades his nostril, he feels there is no one there to catch him, he roars, he passes out.

He wakes up unable to breathe. He coughs and splutters. A heart-attack, he must be having a heart-attack. He somehow gets to the car and drives to the village, finding the surgery, the place where he met Miss Needham, those days seem distant now. She has moved on and the replacement has not yet arrived.

Dr. White sees him immediately. He does some checks. 'Well, every thing is in order. It is a difficult time for ye,' he says, handing him a prescription. 'Take them as you need them. They'll calm you down a bit.'

Gus wanders around the town. People nod at him as he walks along the street, they say things to him, he replies, but knows not what he says. It is nearly eleven.

He sits in The Red Oak. Gus takes three of the tablets and orders a whiskey. Liam shakes his hand and begins a tirade about the local elections next year. Reilly snores on the bar counter.

Gus wanders the road out of the town, along the river where the water is choppy. Numerous boats sit in the pier, dormant, awaiting the next year of summer. Everything is shutting down now for the winter. Everything is becoming darker and more difficult. Now he begins to wish he did live in the old caravan in the wood, on his own, with no one to bother him and he bothered about no one. That would be the ideal solution.

A lamb is stuck in the fence across the road; he wanders across and gets over the wall. The ground is softer in the field, more forgiving to his imprint.

He reaches the lamb and helps it out, pulling it gently away from the wires which seem to obstinately try to keep their prey. He sits on the ground for a long time.

10

Gus drives to the forest, through the winding boreen, in through the trees, their pine needles brushing against the side of the car. 'Goodbye' meanders through the tight car air. In the clearing the caravan stands, untouched since he met the official from the island in the north. It is of no use to him now; his housing application has been refused. But it does not matter anymore.

Outside, the High Nelly bicycle has fallen over. The door swings open in the light breeze. Inside the air is stale and damp. He wanders around, looking at the hard bed, the three-legged chair, the small shower unit. The presses which once contained mini-bottles of ketchup and side-plates. There is a sense of confine, of another little world within a world in the caravan. The windows are a strange, curved plexiglass which present a slightly blurred version of outside. He could stay in here forever.

He sees the old coffee jar, recalling the morning with Miss Kilroy, the fisherman's mug, the first sight of her. She was the one surely. But then at the clinic it had all become so confusing. He cannot follow his thoughts on that any further.

His old hammer on the bed reminds him of work. He has not worked in some time. These days, his former employer spends his days staring blankly at afternoon TV, being fed at regular intervals with a spoon. It was a cruel thought, but McCluskey had been the one that had always boasted of avoiding strokes.

Now his father has departed, and Gus owns the cottage and the field around it, maybe he could try and become a farmer. Renting nine acres, getting a herd number. Living alone in the cottage, after his mother moves in with Stephen and his family, which looks likely now, since Augustus started behaving strange. But a life like that for him seems faintly ridiculous.

A letter had arrived earlier in the morning, advising him he was being investigated by the criminal fraud squad. He had been under observation for some time and the evidence was now at a stage where the department were ready to embark upon a full investigation. He was to attend a hearing in November.

He puts his hand in his pocket and pulls out a crumbled ball of decomposing vegetation. He stares at it for a few moments. The little bouquet. He had given it to neither of his girlfriends. Perhaps if he had, none of this would have happened. He tosses the pile to the floor. He took another large swing of Boggo's concoction from the coke bottle he had brought with him.

He sits on the bed. The coldness rises up through his clothes and he shivers. He takes out his notebook from his pocket and, as he turns the pages, he reads the lines. 'The Belly'. 'The Official and the Nurse'. 'Beautiful mountains, beautiful–'. He stops reading.

He pulls all the pages from his notebook and tears them and the cover into small pieces and throws them onto the ground over the decayed flowers. He checks all the windows. He goes outside and turns the ignition in the Lancer. He takes a roll of 2-inch heavy gauge pipe from the boot. He fits the pipe onto the exhaust. He fits the other end into the vent by the cooker and pushes the oily rag that once performed as a dish dryer around it.

He goes back into the caravan and shuts the door. He takes the remaining pills in his hand and tosses them all in his mouth, washing them down with the rest of Boggo's finest. He lies down on the bed. He becomes drowsy. As he looks up at the ceiling of the caravan, the exhaust fumes cloud the air. He coughs. He begins to drift into a deep, warm sleep. He grapples with his pocket, finds his phone. It slowly comes into focus, he sees the photo of the caravan, still on his screen.

There are no missed calls.

Caravan is Martin Keaveney's fourth book. It follows the novels *Delia Meade* (2020) and *The Mackon Country* (2021) and the short story collection, *The Rainy Day* (2018), all published by Penniless Press. Stage and screen credits include Ireland's national broadcaster RTE and Scripts Ireland Playwriting Festival. He has a PhD in Creative Writing and Textual Studies. Scholarship has been published widely, including at the *New Hibernia Review, Canadian Journal of Irish Studies* and *Estudios Irlandeses*. He was awarded the Sparanacht Ui Eithir for his research in 2016. He works with hundreds of creative writers and literary enthusiasts annually (see more at *www.martinkeaveney.com*).

THE MACKON COUNTRY

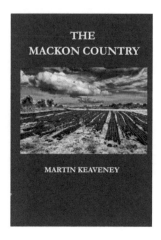

Tommy O'Toole is a talented adolescent from a village at the centre of isolated bog swamps knows as the 'Mackon Country'. He lives in a mobile home with his father Joe, who dreams of completing a half-built house in the field. Nights are spent with Uncle Midnight who plays poker while swilling Dutch Gold and recalling hero stories from his time in Lebanon. When Dad gets caught up in a local ATM robbery, Tommy begins a descent into organised crime.

Purchase *The Mackon Country* at *www.mayobooks.ie* and many other outlets.

DELIA MEADE

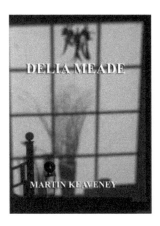

Now the last of Delia Meade's children have married and moved away, she decides to tidy up the little room under the stairs, known as the Glory-hole. Amongst the forgotten toys, worn-out clothes and dusty boxes of photographs, Delia travels through happy and sad decades of her time at 109, Bog Road. *Delia Meade* was published by Penniless Press in 2020.

'An excellent debut.'

Connaught Telegraph

Purchase *Delia Meade* at *www.mayobooks.ie* and many other outlets.

THE RAINY DAY

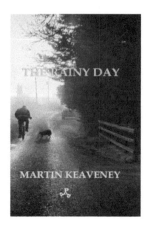

Farmers: young and old, cunning, foolish, greedy, generous, talented and forgotten. These and those belonging to them are gathered in this short story collection, sometimes clearly in Ireland's west, but mostly in an unnamed landscape which shapes those often waiting for that rainy day to come. *The Rainy Day* was published by Penniless Press in 2019.

'*The Rainy Day* [...] will really strike a chord with rural readers.'

Connaught Telegraph

Purchase *The Rainy Day* at *www.mayobooks.ie* and many other outlets.

L - #0063 - 161122 - C0 - 229/152/6 - PB - DID3424459